The Perfect Cowboy

Karen Tucci

True Heart Romance

Dedication

To Dominic :

You're my inspiration for Emmanuel. Your funny quips, sweet thoughts, and empathy are impressive. The strength you've shown since being diagnosed is extraordinary. You've worked hard to be flexible with food accommodations, and you continue to pull your strength from Jesus himself for every one of your infusions. I am so proud of you, and I love you!

Contents

Karen's Other Books:

Stand Alone Books:

When the Dust Settles: A Sweet Romance with a Navy SEAL

G & G Security Series (Coming 2025)

(The characters from When the Dust Settles cross-over in this series)

Operation: Heal my SEAL Book 1

Operation: Find my SEAL Book 2

Operation: Keep my SEAL Book 3

Operation: Train my SEAL Book 4

Second Chance Series:

Starting Over

<u>Moving On</u>

Big L' Ranch Series

<u>The Perfect Kiss: Book 1</u>

<u>The Perfect: Cowboy Book 2</u>

<u>The Perfect Match Book 3</u>

<u>The Perfect Christmas (Holiday Novella)</u>

<u>The Perfect Sheriff Book 5</u>

Best Friends Series

<u>Let Me Carry You</u>

<u>Let Me Marry You</u>

YA Cumberland Christian Prep School Series

The Big Score (Coming 2025)

Chapter 1

The temperature soared, and humidity suffocated her overworked lungs. Sweat rolled off her brow, and her clothes clung to her skin with each stride. The vibration of her feet pounding against the scorching pavement was prevalent in her ears, even overpowering the music blasting through her earbuds. The heat provided her with another challenge she could endure and would overcome.

It had been almost two months since Lily had left California. Though Montana didn't have an ocean, her favorite geographical feature, the breathless mountains and foothills were impressive. The summer months also had the perfect eighty-degree weather during the day. Most importantly, this place seemed safe enough.

Her phone vibrated in her pocket, causing her to halt in the middle of her run. All that surrounded her was wide open land on her left and her right. She knew Big L' Ranch was along this road but wasn't sure how much farther. *You have nothing to worry about.* She tried to convince herself irrational self.

Her hands trembled when she pulled her phone from her biking shorts. Lily shouldn't be nervous anymore. She'd ditched her old phone and number when she moved. The only people who had this number were Violet, her landlord, Amelia from Big L' Ranch, and Raddix, who'd never texted her before. Unfortunately.

> **Hey, Lily, I'm not sure if you're available, but Quinton and I are having a cookout tomorrow. I guess to celebrate that we're back from our honeymoon *woman shrugging shoulders emoji*. We'd like you to join us if you're free. The party starts at 6 pm. Bring your bathing suit.**

A surge of adrenaline shot through Lily's veins. She quickly secured her phone and took off in the opposite direction at her max speed, her mind racing even faster than her legs. *The thought of seeing Raddix again shouldn't have me all school-girl giddy.* She knew dating was not in her immediate future.

Besides, Raddix seemed to close himself off toward the end of their date a month ago. She'd spent three thousand dollars at the bachelor auction to help out the local church. A sweet goodnight kiss seemed like a reasonable request, but the handsome cowboy had stopped holding her hand and *accidentally* bumping his shoulder into hers while they walked through town back to her apartment. Once at her door, he'd only given her a quick peck on her cheek and then hopped in his truck and drove off. He'd been silent since.

Since Lily was a night owl and a borderline, self-made insomniac, she'd spent many nights convincing herself that whatever Raddix's reasons had been for his behavior and for ghosting her now, it was the best for everyone.

An icy chill shot down her spine as she recalled the day she received a single dead rose and a warning note that she'd since memorized right before she moved-err, ran away from California, her only home.

> Your beautiful smile lights up my world, but wearing that flowery dress for anyone other than me and holding another man's hand is wrong. I'll protect you, don't worry. Make sure you change your lock. I enjoyed the cookies on your counter. You're a fabulous baker. We'll be together soon, Sweetheart. In the meantime, if I ever see you with another man, I will kill him while you watch, and then I'll take care of you for not listening.

With that came a ripple of fear throughout her body. The vast open space put Lily on high alert. What if he found her? She was about a mile from her apartment that rested in the central hub of the small town above Violet's flowershop, and Big L' Ranch was the other direction, even more miles. If he found her right now, he could take her, or worse, and no one would ever know.

The music in Lily's ears faded as her sense of safety was irrationally shaken. She silently fretted. *He followed me from California, and he's watching me right now.* Lily ignored the burning in her legs and pumped them harder. *That's not realistic. You know better. What would you tell your patients to do?* With that thought, Lily silently coached herself—*I am safe. He cannot hurt me anymore. He is NOT HERE!* She repeated those statements over and over in her head until she saw the rooftop of her apartment. Pumping her arms even quicker, clearly not believing her own words. She reached the parking lot just as Violet and a tall man who looked vaguely familiar exited the flower shop.

Her sprint turned into a recovery walk. She pulled the earbuds out and stuffed them in her pocket. Resting her hands on top of her head to get control of her breathing, she plastered on the fake smile she'd perfected as the couple greeted her.

"Hi, Lily. You remember Sean, Raddix's dad?" Violet's smile lit up like the sun's rays whenever this man was in her presence. Her petite frame countered his tall, rugged stature, which was cute.

They exchanged cordial smiles since Violet didn't give them time for anything else.

"Looks like you had a great run. Did you make it to the Ranch today?" Violet's cheery voice, something Lily usually welcomed, was hitting her wrong at the moment.

Ugh. I shouldn't have told Violet my goal. Now Raddix's dad might tell him, and he'll think I'm some crazy woman trying to check on him. Playing dumb might work. "Ranch? Do you mean Big L' Ranch? I'd never try to run that far." Hopefully, her expression was convincing and not a look of disgust. She couldn't focus on anything except her heart pounding against her ribs.

"Well, I've got to be going. It was nice to see you again, Lily. I'll be back on Thursday for another order, Violet," Sean stuffed his hands in his pockets and jogged to his truck and sped off.

Once Sean was out of sight, Violet turned her attention to Lily. "What's wrong, you look like a frightened deer running for its life."

Lily forced a half smile. If Violet only knew.

Violet had been trying to get Lily engrossed in the small community, but she'd always declined. After ten minutes of Violet begging, Lily agreed to join her at the diner and meet some of the locals.

"Welcome to Haven Ridge. How do you like Montana so far? Randall, the convenience store/gas station owner, asked as he shoveled a fork full of eggs into his mouth.

"It's perfect." It truly was, but she'd never tell them that she picked this place for its name. She had never heard of Haven Ridge, but she remembered the words she told herself at the time—*you'll be safe here*. Considering God wasn't doing anything to protect her anymore, she had to take things into her own hands. Now that she'd been here to see its beautiful rolling hills, the runoffs from the Missouri River, she knew she'd made the right decision.

Lily was seated next to Cora, Pastor Myles's wife. Violet had shared that the power couple was about a decade older than Lily. Just looking at Cora, with her wrinkle-free, smooth complexion, it would be impossible to tell.

"We've heard so many great things about you," Cora said, her smile wide with bright white teeth sparkling. "I'm glad our weekly visit finally matched up with yours."

"I've never known Violet to exaggerate," Lily laughed, making the joke about herself.

"Oh, stop that," Violet waved her hand, dismissing the comment. "This is Harper, she owns the clothing/consignment shop," the older lady, with sharp eyes, announced with reverence.

Harper's scrutinized look put Lily on edge. "Where are you from?"

"California." Lily took a sip of water, trying to swallow her fear down before any of these folks noticed.

"Funny, you don't look like a Lily."

Lily coughed at the same time she'd taken another drink. Her hand bolted to her mouth and she pushed her chair away from the table just as she sprayed her drink all over the floor in front of her.

Violet handed her a napkin. "Are you okay?"

"Yes, thank you," Lily said as she wiped her mouth and hands. Violet didn't look convinced.

But Lily wasn't about to admit how right Harper was.

Lily liked the idea of making a life here. Even if Raddix never called her again, she could build a new life right here in Haven Ridge unless they found out about her past and ran her out of town, not wanting the trouble.

Chapter 2

"I'm so excited, Raddix. Guess who's coming to the cookout today?" Amelia's singsong voice echoed throughout the barn.

He didn't lift his head from the first milking of the day, "It's too early for guessing games, Amelia, just tell me."

Raddix and Amelia were more like brother and sister rather than cousins. They'd grown up together on this ranch, just like their father's had. Their great-great grandfather erected the main house and put up the Big L' Ranch sign in the eighteen hundreds, which had since had some restoration.

"Lily. She texted late last night asking what she could bring." Amelia grabbed another bucket and a stool. She plopped down next to Raddix, helping him with the chores—a must if they were going to quit early tonight.

His eyes froze on Amelia for a brief second. "Why would you invite her? I told you we haven't seen each other since our date," Raddix barked.

"Sorry-yyy, Mr. Grumpypants. I assumed you were too busy to date since I was gone, so I thought I would repay the favor."

Raddix turned his attention back to the cow he had been milking. "In the future, please don't do me any unsolicited favors."

"What's your problem? She seemed really sweet. I thought you'd be good for each other."

Heat crept up his face as he stared at the milking pail, now nearly full. "I know you've become fast friends with her, and I'm happy for you, really, I am." He paused for a moment and sheepishly returned to his chore. "You know I don't date a woman for long, so I figured why bother? Nothing will come of it."

"Please tell me this doesn't have anything to do with Selena."

Selena had been his only long-term girlfriend back in high school. She'd used him to get close to Dixon Bradley, the quarterback and one of Raddix's good buddies at the time. He'd gotten justice when Dixon had refused to date her once he'd found out what she'd done. Amelia's mom, his Aunt Marilyn, had given him one of her famous, motherly hugs, which he always appreciated, and told him, "Selena is one rejection closer to finding the girl for you."

She still lived at home with her parents and frequented Big L' Ranch a few times a month since Amelia honored the agreement her dad and Selena's dad had made years ago, where the Whittakers provided an unlimited amount of eggs to the Lawrence family while Jeff offered his butchering services to the Whittakers.

Cracking his knuckles, something Raddix always did when he was frustrated or nervous, he responded with an annoyed tone, "No, it doesn't."

That was the truth. Selena didn't have any holds over Raddix. In fact, her evilness hadn't changed any, so the only feeling that kept resurfacing whenever she was in his presence was disgust.

His stomach lurched. Besides him, his primary confidant seemed so smug, so sure of herself. Amelia usually didn't pressure him to date, but against the pushing and prodding, he knew that was coming. He'd never stand a chance.

Amelia's phone blared with an incoming text message. He watched her with hopeful anticipation that someone, *anyone,* needed her somewhere else.

Wiping her hands on her jeans, she pulled her phone out and read her text. "Sorry, but I have to go help Damon with the horses."

"No worries, Dad will be out any minute to help me."

"This conversation is not over, Raddix." Amelia pointed at him before jogging off.

"Whatever you say, Em," he mumbled to himself. It was over as far as he was concerned.

Ever since his dad had told him that he'd seen Lily yesterday, Raddix hadn't been able to stop thinking about her and he didn't like it. This morning, he'd woken before his alarm, and instantly, his mind focused on her. Instead of laying there, letting his thoughts go wild, Raddix had thrown his covers off, not bothering to pick them up from the floor, and trudged to the bathroom. He'd taken only a few minutes to brush his teeth, throw on his jeans, belt, gray t-shirt, cowboy hat, and was out in the barn before the rooster crowed.

There were days on the ranch that ran well into the night. He'd been outside with spotlights tending to calves, helping with births, fixing posts; you name it, Raddix had done it. Though all the births had already taken place for the season, there should be something that would keep him working and not able to attend the cookout.

"Nice work, Son. I'll finish up the bedding for these little beauties. You can head in and get ready," Sean encouraged.

"It's alright, Dad, I can do that. You go get ready." Raddix said, trying to sound upbeat since he knew that his dad didn't want to entertain people any more than he did.

Raddix's mouth opened, then snapped shut when his dad, a man of few words, used his dad's tone with his adult son. "I've got it, Son. Go on now."

He paused. Raddix contemplated whether or not to address whatever issue his dad was having, causing him to speak to his son that way. *What the heck? How much worse could it get?*

"What's with all the tension today?"

The smirk that slowly slid across his dad's face told Raddix that he'd quickly regret his decision to push his dad.

Removing his smirk, Sean stated flatly, "If you avoid dating that girl any longer, you'll lose her. She's a beauty."

"Alright, Dad!" Raddix threw his hands in the air. He knew his dad was right. "I don't need to hear this. I'm outta here."

Sean waved his hand without a word before returning to the bedding chore.

By the time Raddix cleaned himself up, the party had been underway for almost an hour. Needing the extra time to himself, he walked the well-beaten path between his cabin and the main house. The music blared louder the closer he got to the party.

Then, out of the corner of his eye, he saw her—Lily—talking with Amelia and Quinton. One of them must have said something funny. Lily tipped her head with a big smile and laughed. Her blonde locks flowed down her back. *Did she curl her hair for this party, or had she straightened it before?* The tip of his cowboy boot hit a rock or something, causing him to stumble forward. Quickly straightening himself before anyone could see, he looked around at the ground. There wasn't anything there. So much for that familiar path!

He slid behind the other guests, trying to avoid the woman who'd distracted him a moment ago. A small part of him felt guilty for avoiding her. He didn't want her to get self-conscious about him disappearing. But he had his dating rule, and if he was around her too much, he was sure to break it.

The night dragged on. Raddix felt his eyelids starting to droop. He'd spent all his time paying attention to where Lily was so he could go the opposite way. It was exhausting work—not so much physically, but mentally.

He spotted Lily with Violet and his dad. *How could she be so awake?* Looking at his watch, almost nine—his bed was calling his name. Raddix didn't think his dad would embarrass him, but as he had witnessed earlier, his dad was the silent, lethal type. He'd be quiet, learn everyone's weaknesses, and then use them against them.

After ten minutes of talking with Jeff, the ranch's butcher, Raddix had lost track of Lily for the first time that evening. His depleted voice bid those in his immediate surroundings a good night, and Raddix slipped back to his cabin.

He could still hear the faint music from his porch. Leaning up against the railing, his head tip back, as he stared at the picture-perfect sunset with streaks of red. "It'll be another hot one tomorrow," he said, sighing into the night air.

"After the winters here, I never thought anyone would complain about a hot day."

Raddix spun on his heels. Lily. She was leaning against the corner of his cabin, hugging her arms around her middle. His heart hitched slightly. *Lord, help me.* His chest tightened, and a match lit in his belly. Yeah, he was thirty-five but healthy as the little filly he and Damon helped Rocco deliver three months ago. That could only mean one thing—the woman in front of him still affected him like the day they'd met.

Her long blonde hair draped over her tan, toned shoulder. She glowed. He could let himself get lost in her blue eyes. During their date, he'd been close enough to see green speckles. She was a beautiful woman, no doubt.

Stupid rule.

Did she walk all this way just to see me? Raddix tensed at the thought. He leaned against the post holding up the porch ceiling, hopefully looking as casual as her. *Did she suck in a breath?* The last month, he'd frequently wondered if he should ask her out for at least one more date, but he'd talked himself out of it every time.

Lily slowly dipped her head while her petite fingers curled a loose tendril behind her ear. Then, she looked up at him with those big blue eyes; at that angle, he saw the speckles. Raddix's heart skipped. *What the heck was that? Am I having a heart attack?*

Something told him this woman would be trouble for him, but in a good way.

Chapter 3

Her mind raced. Raddix's silence had her wondering if she should have listened to Amelia about trekking to Raddix's cabin to surprise him. His dark sienna-colored eyes pinned her down like she had seen in that cowboy's eyes when he wrangled an excited calf at the Fourth of July carnival.

Leaning against the pole with his ankles crossed, Raddix grinned. Lily swallowed hard, wishing she put an extra swipe of deodorant on before leaving her apartment. He didn't seem happy to see her, but he didn't look disappointed, either.

"Do you think I don't know that look?" She challenged him. Lily saw it most of the time she looked in the mirror, but she wouldn't tell him that she had become the biggest scaredy cat on earth. With good reason, but it was still annoying.

Raising his eyebrows and crossing his arms over his chest to match his feet, Raddix's muscles popped, making her throat go even more dry.

"Pray tell, what look is that?"

"Fear," Lily stated with confidence.

"Fear?" he scoffed, bolting upright. She'd enjoyed the previous pose, but this one wasn't bad either. Though his muscles weren't flexed and popping under the pressure of the position he'd just been in, his t-shirt did little to hide the years of hard work he'd endured on the ranch. Lily fanned herself. This man emitted enough testosterone for at least two men.

Lily shook her head. She stood upright and placed her hands on her hips to contest his stance. *What would he have to fear?* The times they'd been together, he had been funny and confident until he walked her home the night of their date. He had the same nervous look on his face then as he did now.

"Perhaps you're seeing dread, knowing I'll have to walk you all the way back to the main house, and I was hoping to relax for the night. You know I'm an early riser and all." She heard the teasing in his voice.

Playing along, she huffed out a breath. "I'll have you know, one," she held up her finger, "that I don't need you to walk me anywhere. Two," she held up another finger, "I only came here because Amelia told me I should check on you. And three," she held up a third finger, "I'd probably fair better walking back alone anyway. I bet the wild animals see you and have the urge to attack just because." *Especially here, who knows what's out in these woods.* She shook her head free of that thought before her imagination could take flight.

Raddix's lip twitched, clearly holding back a laugh. His hands dropped from his chest. "You're safe here." He took a step toward Lily, but she put her hands up to stop him.

"I will be if you don't come closer. Those animals are probably watching right now, trying to decide if I'm a threat, too. You know, guilt by association and all," Lily chuckled realizing how silly she sounded to someone who didn't know what she dealt with in her brain. Or maybe it was just plain silly, regardless.

Raddix just stared at her. His eyes looked playful, but then a change came over him again. This man was like a chameleon.

"Well, I did as Amelia asked, so I'll be heading out. Bye, Raddix." Lily turned away.

"Everyone always leaves," he mumbled. Fortunately, Lily was an expert at listening to people who mumble.

She paused. Tossing him a look over her shoulder, "It's been my experience that people will leave if they are treated badly or don't feel wanted. You can't put all the blame on the other party."

"What'd you think you're some psychologist or something?" A slow smile pulled at his lips, letting her know that he was still teasing her.

"Nah, I just play one during my free time," Lily countered.

"Funny. I know why you came back here." Raddix's smirk was too handsome to ignore.

"I can't wait to hear this." Lily crossed her arms over her chest.

He pulled the t-shirt stretched across his chest away from his skin. She dragged her eyes from that movement back to his enticing lips and finally settled on his eyes. She'd been had. His knowing smile lit up the darkness around them.

"To see your favorite cowboy," he finished with a grin.

"Huff!" Lily tipped her head back, releasing the tension creeping up in her chest. "You're full of yourself, Cowboy!"

She tossed her hair over her shoulder and took off again. A little faster this time, uncertain that being flirty with the handsome cowboy was a smart idea, albeit fun.

"Hey, wait up!" He jogged beside her and turned backward, continuing to walk since she hadn't stopped. "Seriously, why'd you come to see me?"

"I guess you'll never know now." Lily sidestepped and took off in a quick jog, leaving Raddix alone in the middle of the path she knew she shouldn't have traveled.

The demand for telehealth therapy has risen exponentially in the last few years. When Lily first started her career, she never imagined she'd be working with people all across the country. Sadly, she had to discontinue seeing her previous patients since they would naturally wonder why she'd changed her name and added a bit of dark highlights to her hair.

Fortunately, she'd been working on building her own business for a while now and had a website near completion. She finished it and made it live when she'd first arrived in Montana. She only had five patients but felt blessed to have that many in a month.

"Lily, how am I going to get through this?"

After jotting down a few comments, Lily set her pen down and stared into the camera on her laptop—she wasn't sure when she'd get used to that. She liked looking into people's eyes; they told her a lot. Just like Raddix's had last night. She took a deep breath to clear her head. He was the last thing she needed on her mind.

"Evelyn, it will be hard. Having your husband of thirty-five years walk away without a good explanation must be so difficult, but you can get through it if you let yourself."

Lily paused, wondering if the woman would ask what she meant, as usual. When she hadn't, Lily continued. "Often, people tell themselves they can't do something. You'll need to avoid asking yourself questions you can't answer, like why did he leave? Every chance you get, remind yourself that you are special."

"I pray all the time, Lily. My mind knows God doesn't let anything touch us unless He allows it, but I don't understand why this is happening."

Lily thought that at one time, too. Now, she did the exact opposite of the advice she'd just given. She asked God why He let her situation happen. When she didn't get any answer, she stopped talking to Him.

"Not knowing is the hardest part. But you do know that God loves you. Keep your eyes open, though. There must be a lesson He's trying to teach you through this." She offered more thoughts than she believed herself.

What lesson could Lily possibly need to learn from having a crazy man who wanted to kill her and any man she interacted with?

"I can't imagine what?" Evelyn pulled Lily's attention back to where it should be.

"Only God knows, but if you ask, He'll reveal it. Maybe He wants you to rely on Him and trust Him. I'm not sure, but I know when you persevere through the struggles, you come out stronger than before." She remembered her pastor saying that. Too bad she didn't believe it herself anymore.

"Thank you, Lily. I feel so inspired when we finish talking."

"I'm glad to hear it." *My pastor deserves the accolades right now.* "I'll see you next week. Bye." Lily signed off.

"Finally a break," she sighed to her empty room, exhaustion pulling at her eyelids. Lily tried not to nap during the day, hoping to sleep at night, but that didn't always work out.

After taking a long drink of water, she checked her watch. Today, she was helping Violet in the flower shop downstairs. Throwing on her sandals, she opened the door to find an unsolicited box sitting there addressed to her.

Lily clutched the door frame, realizing she'd stopped breathing. She didn't like the Déjà vu feeling coming over her. Despite the cool breeze today, heat ransacked her body, and sweat formed on her head and under her arms. A wave of nausea assaulted her.

She coached herself aloud, as if she were her own patient, "You are fine. It is just a box. A box cannot hurt you. Don't let your imagination create things that are not real."

"Easy for you to say," her inner voice responded. Was this how her patients felt? Lily gave solid advice that did work, but in the moment, how practical was the advice? Lily empathized even more with her patients.

She heard a door slam. Holding her breath, her eyes darted around, looking for any potential danger. She heard footsteps. Were they coming after her? Each footfall got louder as the culprit approached. When the bell above the flower shop door jingled, she let out her breath, slumping against the doorway, allowing it to hold her weight.

Stepping gingerly over the small box, Lily shut her door and rushed down the stairs, hoping it would disappear as quickly as it had appeared. Lily knew better than that. She'd have to deal with this one way or another. Guilt pricked at her heart. She needed to tell Violet the truth just in case he found her.

Lily shuddered at the thought.

Chapter 4

The flower shop was packed. Granted, it was a small space, so ten people filled this place to its brim. Violet had told Lily that for the last week people from all over had been getting flowers from her. She wouldn't question the Lord's work but wondered about the influx to her shop.

Seeing the smiles on the women's faces as they picked flowers and formed bouquets filled Lily with happiness. Watching the few men choose just the right flowers for their loved ones struck her with a pang of sadness. She'd never have any man do that for her; her pursuer made sure of that.

Lily lifted her hand, acknowledging Sean, Raddix's dad, sitting near the checkout, probably waiting for Violet to help him with his weekly order.

As she looked around, a chill ran down her spine. Lily felt like she was being watched. That had to be her irrational thinking, working overtime again. *You are safe. Don't let your fears rule your life.* She coached herself.

Getting right to work, she asked, "Can I help you," approaching one of the men who looked clueless.

"Oh, please. My wife loves lilacs, but I don't see any."

Lily smiled at this husband's thoughtfulness. "Lilacs are my favorite, too; the purple ones specifically."

"Yes, my wife likes the purple ones, too."

"Well, the white ones, which are right over here, smell the same, so in a pinch, I can get by with them. Do you think your wife could?"

"I certainly hope so."

Lily noticed Sean studying her with a smile on his face. She wondered what that was all about.

She finished up with that customer. Searching around the room for a new one to help, her eyes landed on a man near the corner of the store. He kept looking at her but averted his gaze whenever her eyes connected with his.

Before Violet strode away from the register, in a hushed tone, Lily asked, "Do you know that man?" Lily jerked her head in the man's direction.

"No, but he seems to like what he sees," she wagged her eyes at Lily. "He better hope Raddix doesn't walk in, or he'll go flyin' out." Lily couldn't help but giggle at the image the woman's words produced in her mind.

"I'm sure Raddix would hardly notice, or even care."

Violet let out a muffled laugh. "You're the only one in town who thinks that, Dear."

Lily shook off the uneasy feeling and helped the lady who requested her assistance.

By the time she'd cashed out that customer and three others, the store was nearly empty. Only Sean and Violet remained holed up in the corner, creating a beautiful bouquet.

Stepping toward the door, she intended to leave.

But, movement across the room grabbed her attention. That man was still there? Lily hadn't paid him much attention, and she assumed he'd left. He moved closer, looking like he wanted to ask a question.

Her feet were cemented to the floor. Lily plastered on a smile. She needed to move. "Is there something I can help you find?" Her voice squeaked a little. Hopefully, he didn't realize how creepy he made her feel.

The man's bloodshot eyes were the only alarming feature, but that alone made her skin crawl. Otherwise, he had athletic shorts and a cotton t-shirt. He had sandy blonde hair, and as he inched closer, she could see blue eyes. She couldn't figure out where she'd seen him before, but she knew she had.

Finally, her feet loosened, and she slid behind the counter, banging her hip hard enough to know a bruise was already forming.

He moved closer to the side of the counter. "I'm looking for roses for my girlfriend." His intense stare felt like a cluster of spiders bristling across her skin. He stood way too close to Lily for someone buying roses for his girlfriend. She'd never been so thankful for a counter.

"There are orange roses right by the door." Lily pointed toward the bucket overflowing with bright flowers. *How could he have missed them?*

The man barely looked over his shoulder. "Thanks, but I was looking for red." He strode out the door without another word.

She let out a breath, thankful he was gone.

Once she could no longer see him from her spot, she rushed to the window. Lily looked left and then right. *Where had he gone? People don't just disappear.*

By the time he left, and Lily was back in her apartment preparing for her sessions with clients, she was officially creeped out and hoped she never saw that man again.

Chapter 5

A billowing of dust toward the road caught Raddix's attention. The family had left the first mile of the driveway dirt like it had been from the beginning. Once visitors reached the rod-iron sign of the Big L' Ranch overhead, it turned to asphalt.

Quinton, Amelia, and Emmanuel waited. Emmanuel twisted his little fingers around each other and moved from one foot to the other as he stared at the car. Once it stopped, Quinton urged the little guy to greet their guest, but Emmanuel wouldn't move. At least he wasn't hiding. From the time he'd gotten diagnosed with ASD until very recently, Emmanuel would hide whenever anyone new came around. Raddix quickly tied Duncan and Yoshi's reigns around the post and jogged over just as Lily stepped out of the vehicle.

His jog turned into a slow-paced crawl. What could he do? If he turned back now, it would be too obvious that he was trying to avoid her. *Buck up! You won't date, and that's okay.*

But you want to . . .

"Shut up," Raddix scolded his inner self just as he reached the group.

"Who me?" Emmanuel asked.

"No, Buddy, I was talking to myself. At least he didn't lie to others, just himself, apparently.

"What's going on? I am supposed to take Emmanuel out on Yoshi to check for any more breaks in the posts. Amelia, I'm taking Duncan. I think he feels neglected since you dropped him for Quinton," Raddix chuckled.

"Better he be neglected than me," Quinton retorted.

"What does that mean?" Emmanuel asked innocently.

"You'll figure it out when you're older," Quinton assured him while the adults snickered.

Raddix appreciated the blush creeping up Lily's cheeks. She was adorable.

Quinton cleared his throat, pulling Raddix's attention from the beautiful woman he'd spent too many nights dreaming about yet knew very little about.

Slightly nodding his head, silently thanking Quinton, he realized Amelia had already caught on and was smiling like the Joker. "Well, Amelia began," Raddix didn't like her singsong voice. "Lily has agreed to work with Emmanuel, and it might be nice if you tag along with whatever they do for a little bit until Emmanuel feels comfortable."

Raddix glared at Amelia, who hadn't wiped that knowing smile from her face yet. He said, "I don't know if that's a good idea."

At the same time, Emmanuel yelled, "Yes," drew his arm back, and lifted his leg.

Lily said, "I think that's an excellent idea."

"Well, it looks like it's settled," Amelia cheered. At least Quinton had the decency to send him a sympathetic look.

He and Quinton had grown closer. Raddix may or may not have referred to him as the brother he never had. They fought and shared stories like one would expect, so Raddix didn't hold this against him. Quinton's hands were tied when going against Amelia. Not that he was afraid of her reaction or whipped as some of the ranchhands teased; he loved Amelia with all his heart and wanted to make her happy. He'd convinced Raddix that it would happen to him when he least expected it.

"Do you even know how to ride a horse?" Raddix's unexpected brazen tone surprised everyone.

"Are you mad, Uncle Raddix?" Emmanuel stepped closer to Amelia. She wrapped her arm around his shoulders and quickly removed it. Balancing on the balls of her feet, Amelia got eye level with him. "Do you know how it is difficult for you to handle your emotions; sometimes you yell because your body feels shaky or has that pent up energy we talked about?"

"Yeah."

"Uncle Raddix has that same problem right now, too." The laughter in her voice wasn't lost on Raddix. He snuck a peek at Lily, who was only studying Emmanuel. Why did that make him a little sad? That was her job. She was there to help Emmanuel.

In true Emmanuel fashion, he quipped, "Maybe you should talk to Miss Lily, too. Maybe your pent-up energy will go away then."

"*Talking* may not help Uncle Raddix," Quinton let out a belly laugh as he pulled Amelia to her feet. "I think they are good here."

He was never telling Quinton anything *ever* again. As the newlyweds stalked past Raddix, Quinton whispered, "Make sure my kid doesn't come back knowing how to flirt or kiss women."

Raddix shoved Quinton, not hard enough to hurt Amelia, who was underneath his other arm, but enough to get his point across. "You're one to talk, Man."

"What Quinton meant to say was 'have fun,'" Amelia winked at him.

When he turned around, he saw Lily sitting on the rock wall with Emmanuel, his legs crossed, staring at the wide open space in front of him, talking a hundred miles per hour. Her ability to get Emmanuel to talk so quickly was impressive. Then he heard the tail end of the conversation and realized Lily and Emmanuel had already started bonding over video games and superhero movies.

"Lemme guess, Luigi and Yoshi are your favorites?"

"Hey, how'd you know, Emmanuel sounded excited.

"Your shirt has Luigi on it, and I'm assuming Yoshi is your horse," Lily responded, and Emmanuel shook his head.

"I think I should ride that horse." Raddix turned to see where Lily was pointing.

Raddix howled. "That's Black Jack, and he's mine."

"He's yours?"

"Yes."

"So, you're a grown man in a five-year-old's body, refusing to share."

Dang, when she's sassy, her cute button nose twitches, making her even more appealing.

"Funny, I thought with it being my horse and all, I could decide who rides it," he said wryly. "You're going to ride that one." Raddix gripped her wrist and shifted it toward a mare. "Her name is Apple Jack." Sparks ran through his fingers when he made contact with her skin, causing him to pull back.

"Emmanuel, your uncle wouldn't put me in danger to prove a point, would he?"

"He's right there. Ask him; I don't know what he thinks," Emmanuel said stone-faced.

He loved Emmanuel; always saying whatever was on his mind.

"Apple Jack is the best horse for you. She's kind and gentle, just like me."

Her blue eyes, full of amusement, questioned him. All he could think about was wrapping his hand behind her neck, pulling her flush with him, and kissing her until he couldn't breathe.

"The jury is still out on that one," she said with a flirtatious tone, and then patted his chest, almost undoing him. He crossed his arms over his upper body to prevent himself from acting on his earlier thinking.

Thankfully, Lily's question to Emmanuel pulled him from his dangerous thoughts. "You'll have to show me how to ride because I never have. Do you think I'll be okay?"

"Probably not. It's pretty hard to do. I've been riding for months now, and Uncle Raddix, well, he's really old, so I don't know how long he's been riding."

Dang, Emmanuel sold him out. "Alright, that's enough," Raddix interrupted.

Looking confused, Emmanuel asked, "Enough of what?"

Raddix knelt down and whispered loudly, "You can't tell Lily I'm old."

"Why not? You are."

Her soft laugh struck Raddix. It was beautiful. He placed his hand over his chest like he was stabbing himself with a knife.

"Let's go, Lily." Emmanuel waved her forward. "He does dumb stuff like that all the time."

Ouch. Emmanuel definitely wasn't a good wingman.

Chapter 6

They'd been out for about an hour before stopping to fix part of the fence Raddix found broken. Despite having never ridden a horse, Lily was getting the hang of it. Sort of. She lost her footing when she dismounted and stumbled backward right into Raddix's hard chest. Since then, some tension between Raddix and Emmanuel appeared.

"Lemme try," Emmanuel pleaded when Raddix couldn't get the rope that Emmanuel had tangled untangled.

"Give me a minute, Buddy," Raddix put his hand up, clearly frustrated that he couldn't fix the issue.

Emmanuel sighed but listened. He started pulling at the grass, and Raddix then corrected him for that. Emmanuel sat on the lower rung of the fence. It was counterproductive since it was the spot Raddix needed to fix with the rope for the time being, but it was apparent that Emmanuel was just as frustrated as Raddix.

Placing her hand gently on Raddix's forearm, he froze. His eyes gradually made their way down to where her hand rested. She pulled her hand back. "Sorry. I don't mean to overstep, but he offered to fix his mistake with the rope, but you wouldn't let him. Then he tried to entertain himself with things you didn't want him doing either. It might be in your best interest if you let him try to untangle the rope. That will give you a chance to either help him or do something else that needs your attention."

"Do you over-explain everything all the time?"

"Only when I'm dealing with difficult people." Lily raised her eyebrows and jutted out her hip slightly to drive the point home that he was being a jerk.

She hoped she wouldn't tick him off to the point he convinced Amelia and Quinton to change their minds about her working with Emmanuel. She'd forgotten how much she liked working with people, especially kiddos, in person, and Emmanuel's vibrant personality made her smile often.

"Here, Buddy, do you want to try getting the rope untangled?"

Emmanuel walked over, seeming to have lost some of the energy he had when she first arrived. He grabbed the rope and sat in the field, concentrating on the knot.

"How were you feeling when Uncle Raddix wouldn't let you try."

Crickets...literally.

"Emmanuel?"

"Shh, I have to concentrate. Talk to Uncle Raddix."

Lily didn't get offended easily, and she hadn't now, either. Some of her favorite patients were her neuro-divergent ones. Lily always knew where she stood with them, at least the younger ones.

She stood and walked over to Raddix, who was attaching clips to the other rope. He smirked when she stopped next to him. "He does that to everyone, well, except for me. I'm his favorite."

"Not really," Emmanuel called from behind them, causing Lily to laugh out loud.

Buttoning her lips, she mumbled, "Sorry." She couldn't wipe the smile from her face, though.

She silently watched him attach the clips. His hands weren't as steady as she'd expected, figuring with a ranch this large, he must fix posts often. "What happened?" She pointed toward the broken fence.

"Most of the time, it's the cattle breaking the fence, but this break came from a person."

"How do you know?"

"The boot print was a dead giveaway this time," Raddix deadpanned.

Lily searched Raddix's profile, his concentration on the rope in his hands. "Does stuff like that happen often?"

Raddix shook his head. "The ranch about ten miles east had six cows stolen about a month ago. Amelia felt bad because that ranch had been suffering the last few years. She brought them three of our brand new calves early this year and filled their freezer with one of our cows."

"Amelia is the most generous person I've met." She'd given Lily the rest of the money she needed to buy a date with Raddix at the bachelor auction and refused when Lily had tried to pay her back. It might have been to prevent the nasty blonde from buying a date with him, but Lily preferred to think of Amelia as generous, and Raddix had just confirmed her thinking.

"How do you guys monitor all this land? How far back and over do you guys own?"

"Well, I, sadly, don't own anything, technically. My dad went through a rough period about thirty years ago when my mother died, and my Uncle Jack, Amelia's dad, had my dad sign over his rights to the ranch so the family didn't lose everything."

"I'm so sorry, Raddix. That must have been difficult for you."

"I'm not your patient. You don't need to talk to me like that," Raddix's gruff response stung.

Lily's temper sparked. "You are the most infuriating person I've ever met. Your arrogance is not becoming. I genuinely feel bad that you endured something so horrific and . . . never mind."

His eyes softened. Lily could tell he was struggling with something that probably had nothing to do with her, so she left Raddix to himself.

"How are you doing, Emmanuel?" Lily squatted next to him, resting her chin on her knees."

"Good, I'm almost done." He looked up when Raddix moved toward the broken post and then put attention back on the rope he had almost all untangled. "My dad says that Uncle Raddix is dealing with something every man faces."

"Interesting."

"Yeah, Dad says Uncle Raddix is going to be grumpy and hard to deal with until he figures it out."

Within a minute, Emmanuel announced. "Oh, Uncle Raddix, look." He proudly held up his untangled rope.

The cowboy's eyes gleamed when he smiled at the young man. Lily enjoyed seeing that side of Raddix. *Too bad he couldn't be quiet longer; he might be easier to be around.*

Lily and Emmanuel headed back to the main house when Emmanuel said he couldn't take anymore. He seemed very lethargic and pale. Raddix assured them he'd only be about ten or fifteen minutes behind them.

True to his word, Raddix appeared about fifteen minutes later while she was talking with Amelia and Quinton. They'd shared that Emmanuel hadn't been feeling well for about a month and a half. When his doctor said he was *perplexed* at what the problem could be, he sent a referral to a GI specialist, and Emmanuel was scheduled for an endoscopy and colonoscopy on Friday.

"Oh, goodness. Where do you have to go for that?"

"Bozeman. We have to leave at five in the morning," Amelia admitted, "It's not an ideal time, but he's lost almost twenty pounds in the last five weeks."

"Huh." Lily didn't want to alarm them, so she refrained from saying more.

She watched Raddix secure the barn door and head toward them. He stopped short, probably realizing the importance of the conversation. "What's up?"

"Lily was just about to tell us what that 'huh' she let out meant," Amelia answered his question.

"I don't want to put things in your head."

"Isn't that what a psychologist does?' Raddix interrupted.

She swallowed down her frustration. *Again? What is his problem?*

"Please tell us, Lily. We won't hold you to anything you say, promise," Quinton urged.

"Okay. When I was twelve, I had all the same problems that you're describing. I had the same procedure Emmanuel will have." Lily didn't wish this on anyone. A wave of nausea rippled through her stomach. "I'll pray it's nothing for Emmanuel, but I got diagnosed with Crohn's Disease the day of my procedure."

Amelia gasped, putting her hand to her mouth. "That was just me, it may not be Emmanuel's story. It just sounded eerily familiar."

Emmanuel came back, not realizing anything was wrong, but still, Raddix sat beside him to distract him.

"How was your first session with Lily?" Raddix asked.

"Good."

"She's wild about me, Little Buddy. It's okay if you can tell me everything she said about me."

"Huh? She hasn't mentioned you once." Emmanuel's brows furrowed as he replied.

"Burnnnn!" Quinton cackled, causing Raddix to glare at him.

When Raddix's eyes met Lily's briefly, she noticed that they had softened, and he placed his hand over his heart.

The mock look of shock and hurt invaded Raddix's handsome features. Lily giggled, liking the way Raddix's mouth curved into a smile, making him even more handsome than before. She wondered if his grumpiness was a coping mechanism.

"I should be going," Lily announced, standing. "Don't worry about anything until you know for sure. If I can be of help, please let me know."

"Thank you, Lily," Amelia and Quinton said at the same time.

Lily stopped in front of Emmanuel. "I hope you feel better, Emmanuel. I'll see you next week." The little guy just waved his hand in acknowledgment.

"I'll walk you to your car," Raddix offered Lily.

"Thanks." Looking back at the trio, Lily waved. "Bye."

"How long have you had Crohn's?"

"Seventeen years." Lily bounced off his shoulder. "If you wanted to know how old I was, you could have just asked."

His cheeks turned red, letting Lily know he'd been busted. "I know you wanted to know our age difference to see if it played in our favor or not since you are old." She enjoyed playing off of Emmanuel's earlier joke about his age.

Once they reached her car, Raddix's hand overlapped hers when they both reached for the door handle. A jolt of energy zapped her fingers, and she pulled back quickly.

She swallowed, "Thank you."

He nodded his head as he opened the door. Leaning his forearm on the top of the door frame, he looked like a model posing as a cowboy. She found the nod and the lean two of the sexiest things a man could do. Why? It was nonchalant. He was so confident and gorgeous . . .

Get your thoughts under control. You can't date him, so don't ogle him.

"So, I was thinking... well, would you...um..." Raddix started and stopped. Lily's eyes widened, encouraging him to continue. She found him absolutely adorable when he got flustered. "Maybe we could grab dinner tomorrow at the diner?"

"Like I said, I have Crohn's, so I don't eat out unless I absolutely have to. Besides, I think you might be too grumpy for me," Lily admitted.

"Oh, right. That's why we didn't eat out on our date." The realization was evident in his tone. "I'm sorry," Raddix pressed on his knuckles. Pop. Pop. Pop.

Lily found it interesting that he disregarded her comment about him being grumpy. "I could make you dinner at my place, and then we could go on a walk through town if you'd like."

He loomed closer. "I'd really like that. I can be at your house between six and six-thirty. Does that work?"

"Sure." She half shrugged, hoping she didn't show just how excited she was that Raddix asked her out again. "I'll see you tomorrow night." Lily started her car and pushed the power button for her window just as Raddix shut her door. The muscles in his forearm bulged when he squeezed the door.

"I want to get home before it gets dark, but I'll see you tomorrow," Lily said, putting her car in reverse. She smiled at the handsome man still hanging on to her door.

His eyes glistened, "Well, Cinderella, you better get home before you turn into a pumpkin."

"You better get going, you handsome stallion, before you turn back into a mouse."

His thick throat bobbed when he threw his head back and belly laughed. "So you think I'm a handsome stallion. That's good to know." He winked. "I'll see you tomorrow, Princess." Raddix double tapped his hands on the inside of the door.

She'd spent most of the drive home smiling like a giddy teenager in love. *Love*? Definitely not. *Crush*? Maybe.

Chapter 7

"Handsome!" Amelia assured Raddix. "Roll the window down on your way to get Lily, so some of that cologne will wear off." She waved her hands in front of her face.

"You've always liked my cologne," he cried, smelling himself, hoping it didn't bother Lily. Nerves pricked at his chest. *I shouldn't be going on this date.* He pulled a royal blue Henley shirt over his head and left the top two buttons undone.

"Yup, I like salt on my fries too, but I don't pour the whole shaker on one serving." Amelia's voice, sarcastic.

Raddix didn't dignify her with a response. Maybe he had splashed on a little too much, but there wasn't anything he could do about it now. He faced Amelia with his arms spread out, silently asking how he looked.

"Gorgeous."

He crossed his arms over his chest. "Women are gorgeous, not men."

"You use your adjectives, I'll use mine," Amelia brushed off his comment.

"Look, before I forget. You need to talk with Alex and Allie. They haven't started harvesting the silage yet. If they don't get it all picked and chopped, we'll have to buy more supplemental food for the calves this winter."

"Okay. Don't worry about it. I'll have a talk with them. You just focus on having fun." Amelia nudged him into the kitchen where every family member, except for Rocco, Renee, and their kids, who were on a well-deserved vacation, whistled or cheered at him, commenting on his dark jeans and clean cowboy boots.

"Bye, Uncle Raddix. Have fun." Darlene, Damon's youngest, squealed.

"Does Miss Lily need to help you be more flexible, too," Emmanuel asked, causing Quinton and Jeff to choke on their drinks.

Pointing at the adult table, Raddix growled. "Not a word." Jeff held his hands up in surrender but hadn't wiped the smirk off his face.

Raddix rushed out the door. "Bye. Don't wait up."

He could see why people chose to talk with Lily. She was a great listener and usually only offered advice or her opinion when asked. Mostly, she just asked questions, which made Raddix think more.

She was also a fabulous cook. Lily had made everything from scratch, just like Carolyn and Cash. The homemade lasagna noodles mixed with the sweetness of her tomato sauce and the moist cheese filling melted in his mouth. The work she had to go through just to eat was insane. Making her own tomato paste took her three to four hours just for the cooking process. That didn't include the time it took to boil and deseed over thirty tomatoes. Then, she needed the same amount of tomatoes to make the sauce. He got tired just listening to her describe that. Then, she told him that she needed seven days to make sourdough bread. His mind rushed to Emmanuel. Thank goodness the ranch had full-time cooks. He wondered how Lily found the time to make her food, let alone eat.

Before Raddix could walk through the town with this beautiful woman on his arm, he needed to help her clean up.

"I tried to get here before Violet closed up for the night, but I guess I'll have to give you roses next time."

Lily dropped the plate she was washing in the sink. Fortunately, it didn't break, but he watched the color drain from her face, making his stomach drop. "I'm sorry, did I say something wrong?"

"Don't worry about it," Lily said, shaking her head. "If a guy brings me roses, the date ends there."

"Well then, I'm glad Violet closed because I was starving," he chuckled. "But pray tell, what type of flower should a guy bring the pretentious doctor if Roses aren't welcomed?"

Lily picked up the sprayer on the sink and doused Raddix's shirt. "First of all," she said, pointing a sudsy finger his way and creeping into his space,

"I don't think I am better than anybody else. In fact, the best thing for a guy to bring on a date is the best version of himself. I don't want flowers because he should bring them on a first date or because he thinks it will help with the end of the date." She poked him in the chest.

Heat crept up Raddix's neck, and he engulfed her petite hand with his. "I wasn't insinuating that, I promise." Raddix took a step back now. Lily, all sixty-four inches of her, was starting to scare him.

"Second of all, it's been my experience that when someone says they don't like something, it's because something in their mind, usually a bad memory or event, is associated with that item, so when you accuse them of being pretentious, or otherwise, they may snap at you."

"Duly noted. I am sorry." Raddix slowly returned to the drying rack when Lily started washing the dishes again. "Do you want to talk about whatever you've associated with the "R" word that I'll never utter again?" he asked, wiping the plate and setting it in the cupboard overhead.

The little pull at her lips told Raddix that she must have forgiven him or, at the very least, found him somewhat funny.

"No, thank you."

"Is that normal?" Raddix questioned.

"What?"

"A counselor who doesn't like to talk about themselves." Raddix dried the last plate and put that away.

"Yes, it can be."

"That's kind of hypocritical, isn't it?"

Her eyes bore into him again. Was it going to be the water again or the finger in the chest? Neither sounded very appealing right now. But then she surprised him.

"Maybe. However, people recruit my services to talk and get help. I don't force anyone to talk to me."

"Good point." Raddix hung the dish towel on the stove handle to dry. "Just so you know," he straightened to his full height and stepped within an arm's length away, "if you ever want to talk to anyone, I'll be a good listener."

"Really? It's my experience that men try to fix everything, and listening is the last thing they actually do."

Raddix guffawed. "I guess you'll have to give me a chance to find out."

Without hesitating, Raddix reached behind his head and pulled his shirt completely off. He liked the blush high on Lily's cheeks and her slackened jaw that she couldn't retract quickly enough to avoid him seeing it.

"Uh, you can't walk around town shirtless; you'll have a target on your chest for all the single ladies and maybe some of the married ones, too." She let out a belly laugh. "I've seen the way Willow, Harper, and Val stared when you entered the diner a couple of weeks back."

He studied her. She pulled on her shirt and shifted from one foot to the other before she grabbed the cloth from the sink, stalked by him without even looking his way, and began scrubbing the table.

"Yeah, I saw that too, but do you know what I didn't see?"

"What?" she asked, continuing to scrub her table without looking up.

"Your eyes."

"What?" She snapped.

He moved next to her, and she stiffened. Raddix reached over and gently placed his hand on top of her soft, silky fingers, stopping her hand.

"Do I make you nervous, Lily?" His breath pushed a section of her hair forward. He slowly pulled her hair over her shoulder, gently grazing her cheek. When she shivered, the urge to pull her close and warm her up pulled at Raddix.

He didn't. These uncharted feelings didn't sit well with him. Would he be able to walk away from Lily when they met his dating quota?

"Would you mind drying my shirt? I'll throw on my sweatshirt since the doctor can't handle a bare-chested man."

"I'm not that kind of doctor." She called to his back before she returned the cloth to the sink.

"Is this better?" He tugged the hem of his sweatshirt down to his waist.

"I suppose that depends on your definition of better."

Raddix let out a low whistle. "My, my doctor, are you flirting with me?"

"Keep dreaming." She grabbed his shirt and stalked down the hall, likely putting it in the dryer for him.

"Every night," he whispered to himself.

Chapter 8

"I never thought I'd live in a small town," Lily declared as she and Raddix walked the streets of Haven Ridge, the place she now called home.

"This is only a small town based on people, one's mind you, who share their unsolicited opinions with you all the time, so you'll need to mentally prepare yourself for that if you haven't already. The Troublesome Trio will be the biggest culprits."

"Who? I haven't met them yet."

"That's surprising. Violet's good friends with them. Beware. They are three ladies who appear to be harmless grandmas, but they meddle in everyone's business. They are super sweet, so people don't mind it, and they mean well."

"Interesting."

Raddix brushed his shoulder against her, sending a tingling sensation to her fingers. "When it comes to land, Montana is not small, but only a few own a lot of it. Amelia recently acquired even more land when Mr. Banks died, leaving his adjacent land to her."

"Why'd he leave it to her?"

His kids didn't want anything to do with the ranch, so after his wife died, he changed his will and left it all to Amelia. We assume it's because Amelia helped Mr. Banks with everything up until the day he died. She now owns the two hundred fifteen acres and his house."

"Wow. Did she hire more ranch hands to help?"

Raddix kept bumping into her as he walked, grazing his fingers with hers every time. If she were bolder, she would just grab his hand next time and lace her fingers through his, but what if it was really an accident? *Nope. once, maybe twice, is an accident. It's been five times.*

Disappointment flooded her body when Raddix stuffed his hands in his pockets. *That's for the best. You can't be dating him anyway, especially since you care about him. You don't want to see anything happen to him. SHUT UP!* She couldn't argue with her inner self—it had developed a fear that lied to her daily.

Lily walked into the same hard chest she'd silently admired earlier in her apartment. Her palms rested on his chest, causing the most thrilling tingling sensation she'd ever felt. Raddix, who, at some point, had turned and faced her spoke with a deep, concerned tone. "Hold up, Little lady. What's going on in that pretty mind of yours that you missed everything I said the last few minutes."

"Nothing I'm willing to share right now."

"Okay," he held the end of the word out a few beats. She felt bad for making the situation awkward.

"How about you tell me about the box that was delivered to your house and why you looked like you just saw the Grim Reaper?"

"How'd you know about the box?" It was at that moment Lily realized the sun had slipped away and the moon shone in the sky. She hadn't felt safe in months, always staying in lit areas when she had to be out after dark, which she made sure wasn't often.

"A man never reveals where he gets his information."

"Actually, a *man* never hides things from his... his..."

"His what?" Raddix's smug smile was irritatingly stunning. But he was just a flirt. He'd waited a month to ask her on a second date, which he probably wouldn't have, but Amelia forced them together when she invited her to the cookout and then again during Emmanuel's first session with her.

"Never mind." Thankfully, he didn't push her this time. As they reached the park, she froze. It didn't have bright enough lights. Things were always scarier in the dark. She hated that her sense of safety had been shaken. Walking next to Raddix should have been enough to make anyone feel safe, yet she felt exposed and naked. The desire to run home and hide under the covers for the night like usual sounded like the best course of action.

"My dad was worried about you. He said a woman never looked that scared unless she had a maniac ex-boyfriend."

"It turned out to be a banana bread from Cora."

"Ah, Cora is known for leaving treats at people's door." Raddix cupped Lily's elbow. "If you want to turn back, that's fine with me."

Could he sense her discomfort? "Okay. Thank you." Lily needed to talk about something else, which always helped her clear her mind.

"Tell me," Lily clasped her hands behind her back as they strolled along, "why are you single?"

"Why are you?"

"No deflecting. I'm not judging you. Just trying to get to know you," Lily tried to assure him.

Raddix stared inside the dinner windows as they passed by. He wrapped an arm around her shoulder, turning her toward the window. "See those ladies sitting in the back booth?" Lily nodded. "Those are the Troublesome Trio. They're probably cooking up something big as we speak."

"Let's get out of here then before we give them ammunition."

They scurried along the road, and she repeated her question.

"I don't date women more than three times," Raddix admitted.

"Never?"

He shook his head, avoiding eye contact with her.

"There a story behind that, care to share?" Lily asked. When he didn't respond, she placed her hand on his forearm, stopping him in his tracks. "Whoever she was—the one who broke your heart—she's an idiot."

A smile reached his lips, and her heart soared. How could this man have such an effect on her in such a short time? She had to work harder and prevent these feelings from happening. She couldn't allow a demented, crazy creep to bring him any harm. *It's a good thing he doesn't date women more than three times. Maybe that will prevent me from liking him any more than I already do.*

"There's more to it than an old girlfriend." His eyes blazed with desire. He wanted to kiss her. If his eyes hadn't told her that much, his gaze honed in on her lips confirmed it in her mind. She wanted to kiss him just as badly. His full lips were beckoning her. *What would one little kiss hurt?* Rationally thinking, she'd moved miles away from danger. She was safe in Montana. Looking at Raddix's strong arms, she knew he'd protect her physically, maybe not her heart, but that could be dealt with another time.

When she nibbled on her lower lip. Raddix clenched his jaw. She moved forward, grabbing onto the hem of his sweatshirt. "This isn't safe."

Raddix cupped her cheeks, tilting her head slightly up toward him. "What isn't safe, Sweetheart."

Lily's heart beat frantically out of control, and she pulled away, ripping her from what would have been their first kiss, one she'd been thinking about for a long time. "Never call me that." She tried to soften her gruff order, "Please and thank you."

"Do you want to share your story?" Raddix lifted his eyes, revealing a couple of lines on his forehead.

"No. I wouldn't want to bore you."

Raddix dared to step closer; she found his bravery impressive. "Don't ever bring the hated flower that starts with "R" and never call you sw— well, you know."

"Yeah, please never say that word in my presence," she interrupted him.

Raddix stepped closer and rested his hands on her hips. "Is this okay?"

Lily's cheekbones hurt from the smile filling her face. She dipped her head to the side and whispered, "Yeah."

Placing his finger under Lily's chin, he lifted it until their eyes met. "Lily, I don't know what skeletons are in your closet, but I'll be here for you if you need me."

"As long as it's tonight or our next date since that would be our third."

"You're already thinking about another date, huh?" The smile in his voice warmed her heart.

Before Lily could respond, she heard a high-pitched voice, like nails scraping down the chalkboard, summoning Raddix. As the woman got closer, Raddix gripped a little tighter on her hips, letting her know he wasn't impressed.

"Who is that."

He let out a sigh and half chuckled, "An idiot."

Chapter 9

"Calm down. It can't be that bad," Damon urged Raddix as they mucked the stalls.

"How can I, Man? Selena acted saccharine sweet, convincing Lily she needed therapy until Lily agreed to start seeing her."

"Well, doesn't that woman need some help?"

Damon wasn't wrong, but Selena never played fair. What if she painted Raddix in a bad light?

"She does but she doesn't need to get the help from my..." Raddix refused to finish his sentence.

"Your what?" Damon smiled knowingly.

Refusing to confirm or deny his suspicion, Raddix shoved his fork into the hay with more force than necessary.

"Look, you've gone on two dates. Based on your own calculations, you only have one more date with Lily, and then you're maxed out, so why not stop now? Is there a reason you want to keep seeing her?"

Raddix couldn't admit to the single dad whose wife left him that maybe this woman, Lily, might be worth a fourth date or more. *Absolutely not. You don't need that kind of headache. What am I thinking?*

"I'm sure Lily's a smart woman and can see right through the people who lie to her. She'll tell Selena that she can't work with her after a few sessions of listening to her nonsense."

"Ya think? Selena is so sneaky." Raddix stuck his pitchfork in the hay and rested his forearm on the top of the handle.

"I do."

Raddix received a text at the same time his ringer alerted him to a call. He answered, "Hello."

"Hi, Raddix. It's Lily. I'm so sorry to call you." Her out-of-breath, worried tone had him on high alert. "I opened my door to go for my run, and there's a dead cat on my doorstep."

"How do you know it's dead?"

"There's blood all over it," Lily murmured.

Raddix shook his head. "That's probably a good indication. Did you call the police? This feels weird."

"No, I called you."

His chest puffed out, realizing that Lily must trust him if she called him. He had to help her. "I'll be there as soon as I can."

"Thank you."

He explained the weird situation to Damon, who also expressed that he thought it was weird for Lily to find a deceased, bloody cat on her doorstep. "Even more telling is that she called *you.*" Damon's emphasis wasn't lost on Raddix. While listening to Damon give him advice, he read a text from Amelia.

> **There's another break in the fence. Maybe we should call Sheriff McDugal? This is getting out of hand.**

> Let's see the damage first, and then we can discuss the next steps. Can Quinton check it out? Lily called, and she found a dead cat on her doorstep.

> **WHAT?! You need to go help her.**

> Hence why I asked if Quinton could check out the fence.

> **Sure, I'll send him out now. Let us know about your situation when you get back.**

The cat had shaken Lily. Raddix wondered if it had anything to do with the story behind why she wouldn't accept roses or the reason she doesn't like to be called sweetheart. He hoped not, but there was no way of knowing if she didn't open up to him.

"Do you have any clients today?"

"No more. I'd been in session." She didn't dare tell him it was with Selena since he was altogether against her taking Selena on as a client. "I walked her out, and nothing was there. I changed to go for a run—maybe it took three or four minutes—then I opened the door, and there it was."

"If you want to go for a run, I can drive alongside you so you feel safe."

"You'd do that?" For a brief second, he thought he'd broken one of her walls down.

"I never offer anything I'm not willing to do," he said with the same tenderness he heard Jeff and Quinton talk to their wives. What was happening to him? He wasn't ready for these feelings.

Fortunately a text from Amelia pulled him from his thoughts.

Is everything okay with Lily?

Yeah. She's shaken up but will be fine.

Invite her over for dinner.

When she accepted, he offered to go on a run with her, telling her to pack a bag and she could shower at his cabin before dinner.

He worked hard every day of his life, but apparently, he needed to work his heart a bit more because Lily was barely sweating, and he thought he was ready to die. "Can we take a break?" His heavy panting made him vulnerable.

"Sure thing, Cowboy. Give me the bag."

Raddix refused.

"Looks like you're the strength, and I'm the endurance. We're a pretty good team." Lily's eyes widened, probably realizing how that sounded. "I didn't mean we were a team, like a couple, or anything, I was actually trying to point out in a nice way that you really should work your heart more because your strength, as appealing as it is, won't be enough to keep you healthy." She slapped her palms against her face.

Raddix gently pulled her to him, noticing her stunning blue eyes with green flecks radiated by the sun's rays. "You are adorable when you ramble." He noticed her chest heaving now. "I don't think your heavy breathing has anything to do with the run, you like me, admit it." He couldn't help but fool with her.

"I plead the fifth." Lily sounded flat, something abnormal for her.

"I'm glad you find my strength appealing and all." He flexed his bicep and smirked. Flirting with her had become his favorite pastime.

She hip-checked him. There were two problems with that. One, she was about a third of his body mass, so he barely flinched, and two, she was about a foot shorter than him, so her mark landed more on the side of his upper thigh and not his hip.

"Let's be real, you are a handsome man," she acknowledged. "Did one relationship back in high school really scar you that badly?"

Raddix hated telling this story to anyone, but it felt different telling Lily. She was a psychologist. Would she be examining him all the while he told his story? Would she tell him he was wrong for thinking what he does or acting a certain way?

"I won't judge. I won't even offer a single comment unless you ask for it."

"You must have been reading my mind, he admitted, a little embarrassed.

Lily smiled, jolting him back to reality. "Okay, I'll tell you, but we have to start walking because I don't think I could share this and have to look at you too."

He opened his mouth to explain his off comment, but she quickly interrupted him. "I get it, trust me."

Raddix told Lily about the storm that had taken his mom from him when he was five. Lily's tender palm on his forearm when he told her about the tree coming through the ceiling, pinning his mom and him down, enticed the feelings that he'd pushed down and ignored for decades. Could he show Lily that he cared about her? He didn't know if she planned on sticking around. But he could deal with those feelings another time.

The part that no one ever talked about was his dad's actions during the accident. "You'll never see my dad take his shirt off, and if you touch his back, he'll jump."

"Why?" The genuine concern in her voice stirred even more feelings in Raddix.

"He saved me." Raddix's silence was met with Lily's gasp. "The fire burned and scarred his back."

She cupped his forearm, stopping him in the process. "I'm glad he did."

That was not what he'd expected. Everyone who knew the story always said the typical things: *I'm sorry, You're lucky he saved you, I can't imagine what he's going through.* He'd stopped listening to the statements long ago, but Lily spoke about her feelings, not about his or how he should feel. She was glad that his dad had saved him. What did that mean?

"He's punished himself for not being able to save my mom, too."

"I bet. From my experience, he's lucky to be alive and sober."

"That's only thanks to my Uncle Jack." Raddix didn't want to share anymore. That was his dad's history.

"So Selena has nothing to do with it? You're not harboring feelings for her?"

Raddix bent over laughing. "Heck no!" he declared, meeting her gaze. Was she studying him to see if he was being truthful?

The sun blinded him in this direction, but he could still see the outline of her immaculate face, clear, porcelain-like skin, and the sun's rays produced a halo-like feature over her head at this moment—very fitting. Was it possible God sent Lily to him? Were they meant to be, or was this all happenstance?

Suddenly, Raddix pulled Lily into his chest, and they stumbled onto the dirt shoulder as a car, one he'd never seen before, zoomed past them, almost clipping Lily. It would have killed her, no doubt.

"Are you okay?" The torment in his voice even pierced his ears.

"Yeah, what the heck was that?" Lily rolled off Raddix's chest and wiped the pebbles jammed into her palms on her running shorts. Hopping to her feet, she extended a hand to help Raddix up. He smirked as they thought about pulling her right back onto him since there was no way *she* was going to lift *him*, but he obliged. To his surprise, she was pretty strong, and he told her so. When she made goalpost arms, she revealed hidden toned muscles that only added to her appeal.

Lily wiped the dirt and pebbles off his arms and shoulders with his shirt that he'd tucked in his shorts long ago. "Thank you. I can't imagine who that was. Usually, the only traffic we have around here is from those on the ranch. Let's get you there so you can clean up."

Chapter 10

"Thank you so much for inviting me, Amelia. Everything was wonderful, Carolyn and Cash. I know how much work you do. If there is a next time, I'll have to bring my homemade banana cream pie."

"Pie? Can I have some?" Damon's kids all asked at once.

"There isn't any tonight," he replied shoving a fork full of steak in his mouth.

"Sorry," Lily mouthed to Damon, who gave her a dismissive wave with the hand holding his fork.

"Will there be a next time?" Damon questioned despite the glare Raddix bore into the man's skin. "I mean, it's not like this is date number three since Amelia invited Lily here, right?"

"Well, Raddix, that is a great question." Lily rested her laced fingers underneath her chin, waiting for his response.

Her soft eyes stared at him, and her full lips begged him to kiss her. He couldn't let her taunting smile get the best of him. He leaned closer to her, mimicking her hand position, and in the deepest, sexiest voice he could pull off, he asked, "Do you want to have a third date?"

Satisfaction filled his chest when her face turned at least three different shades of pink, and she began to stutter when he feather-tipped his fingers across her cheek. The interaction seemed way too intimate for them, especially in front of every adult he respected at the ranch, but he couldn't let Lily get away with thinking she'd gotten the best of him.

"I don't think you could handle a third date." Lily winked at him, and now he felt his face heat up.

He cracked his knuckles, hoping no one paid him any attention, but that was too much to ask for in this family. Jeff, Damon, Amelia, and Quinton's eyes bore into him, knowing his inner struggle. Damon, the grinning fool, thought Raddix's turmoil was funny. Hopefully, one day, he could repay the favor.

With his elbows resting on the table, one palm resting on top of his other hand, Raddix stared at the kid's table. Emmanuel hadn't eaten anything at dinner, and the more fragile he got, the more Raddix worried about his little buddy. Amelia and Quinton hadn't forced him to eat, but they pushed the fluids after they had to take him to the hospital for dehydration.

Raddix's attention was only being pulled back when Lily touched his leg. "Are you okay?"

"Just worried about Emmanuel."

"I understand. You guys will have answers soon." He appreciated her reassuring words. Once again, she didn't make him feel stupid for his thoughts or feelings, she just supported him. Interesting.

"Tell me again about that car." Katy, Jeff's wife, asked, sounding troubled.

"Yeah. Tell us more about your heroic moves, too." Cash piped up. Many confused looks peered his way.

He shrugged. "When I went to the diner earlier, I heard Hazel telling the *girls* (by *girls*, he meant the over seventy gossip group) how she saw Raddix rescue Lily in a heap on the side of the road."

Raddix ignored Cash. *For seventy, that woman had hawk eyes or, more probably, binoculars.*

"It was black." Raddix began. "I've never seen it before. It came barreling down the road, hugging the shoulder instead of going across the yellow line to give us room." Raddix paused. "I mean, the wind alone as it passed was like an eighteen-wheeler going by. I don't know." Raddix shrugged in frustration.

"The sun was too bright and shining just so that I couldn't see a license plate or get the make of the car," Lily added, sounding disappointed.

Ten minutes later, the parents dismissed their children to play downstairs in the homeschool area, but Emmanuel stayed with his forehead pressed against the table before Amelia got him up to go to bed.

Before leaving the kitchen a few minutes later, he asked, "Miss Lily, will you please come to the camera appointment with me on Friday?"

"If that's okay with your parents, I wouldn't miss it for the world."

"Of course. It's alright. Thank you," Amelia said.

"Yes." Emmanuel's weak voice tore Raddix's heart out. He hated seeing him so thin and feeble.

After cleaning up, Damon hollered at Raddix and Lily's backs as they crossed the threshold leading to the enclosed porch, "Have fun, you two." He pumped his eyes when Raddix turned and faced him. Instinctively, Raddix picked up the dishtowel lying on the counter, balled it up, and chucked it at Damon.

Before the door shut, he heard the room erupt in laughter. He was glad they all found this funny. Raddix's interest in Lily had piqued exponentially, and he knew that meant trouble.

How could he walk away from this woman after one more date?

Chapter 11

"This is the most beautiful sight," Lily stared at the sky as she and Raddix lay on a flat section of the barn roof, staring at the sky. "I can see why they call Montana Big Sky Country."

"It's stunning," his husky voice grabbed her attention. When she turned, he was staring at her.

Oh, my goodness. Lily pressed her laced fingers resting on her chest deep into her stomach, hoping to prevent the butterflies from taking flight—no such luck.

"You need to stop flirting with me, Raddix. If I only get one more date with you . . . you're not playing fair."

He turned onto his side and rested his head into the palm of his hand. "I'm not following."

"Do you normally lead girls on?"

"Whoa, what do you mean? How am I leading anyone on? I rarely kiss any of my dates, and if I go on a second date, I tell the girl that I'm not looking for a commitment." The indignation in his tone made Lily feel bad for saying anything. He was right. He had taken weeks to reconnect with her after their first date, and during their last date, he'd let her know that he doesn't go beyond three dates.

If Lily were being honest with herself, like she told her patients to do, she'd have to admit that she liked the cowboy, and the idea of only one more date didn't sit well with her.

"Sorry, I didn't mean to upset you. I guess this is a *me* problem." *Shut up! Why did I say that?* All she needed was for Raddix's ego to get any more inflated.

"A *you* problem, huh?" Raddix's grin made her stomach feel hollowed and excited, the same way it does when riding a roller coaster, just before the coaster drops over its first hill.

"If you're telling me the truth, then it sounds like you're a pretty standup guy. That's impressive."

"What can I say? I'm good like that. Wait?! *If I'm telling you the truth?* What reason do I have to lie to you?"

"What reason does anyone have to lie?" She countered.

He rubbed his stubble, "Do you always answer a question with a question."

"Does it seem like I do?" He lifted his eyebrows and gestured with his hand toward her since that was exactly what she'd just done . . . again. "Sometimes. It's an occupational hazard."

He shook his head, grinning, making her enjoy this time together even more. He was just fun to be around. Maybe they could just hang out after their three dates as friends. *Who are you trying to kid?* Lily couldn't even fool herself into thinking this wasn't something more, for her, at least.

"How do the women take it when you tell them you're not seeking a commitment?"

Raddix let out a huff of breath, clearly a little uncomfortable, but she was used to seeing that with her patients until they got comfortable baring their souls to her. "Some take it well. When we see each other in town, we can chat; for others, I have to call Sheriff McDugal. One of them thankfully moved away a few weeks later."

"Wow. That must have made you feel like hot stuff?"

"Not really. Relief is the only word I could use to describe the joy when she moved away."

Lily chuckled. "You know, we've had our second date, and you haven't directly told me about this commitment deal yet." *Stop flirting with him.* Something within her couldn't stop.

"Do you want me to?"

No! Was it possible he'd change his mind? Would she ever be free to date again? She cleared her throat. "I'm good. We talked about it enough that I get it." She smiled, hoping to keep her feelings close to her heart. "I won't pose a threat. Sheriff McDugal won't have to send me packing."

"You've heard all about my dating habits," Raddix began. "What about you? Did you break someone's heart back home when you left?"

"No. Well, I don't know." Her heart darkened, matching the blackness of her tone. She knew the sick stalker wasn't brokenhearted; he was clearly mentally unstable and alone in the world. She thought of poor River. She remembered the sadness in his voice and eyes when she FaceTimed him to break things off, not daring to be seen with him again. At least she'd told him the real reason. He'd begged her to stay, and he'd protect her, but she wouldn't put that kind of target on his back. It was important for her to remember that now. As much as she liked River, the feelings she noticed swirling inside her for Raddix were more prominent.

"Is the good doctor going to tell me a story?" Raddix chuckled, nudging her shoulder with his palm.

"I'm not a great storyteller. How about you tell me more about my new home and any *idiots* I should be aware of."

She dared look at his handsome face. Thanks to the moonlight, she could only see the glints of his strong, chiseled jaw, but she didn't miss the hurt that filled his eyes.

"There's only one idiot if we use *your* definition from our second date." Raddix rolled back over and stared at the bazillion stars. "Long story short, she's a nasty, mean person. She's a person people want to follow to either be cool or to avoid being her target. Amelia didn't care about any of that, so Selena made it her mission to bring Amelia down. Do you know she even tried to get to Quinton when he first came to town just to keep him from falling for Amelia? I know you can't tell me if you've started seeing her, but please watch out. She is evil."

I think I saw a glimpse of that at the auction. Some of those girls didn't seem to agree with Selena, yet they continued to do what she told them."

"Uh, huh. I must admit that I loved the look on Selena's face when Quinton dropped out of the auction, crushing her dreams of buying a date with him. Then, watching him propose to Amelia—it was epic. I know I shouldn't relish in other's misery, but she deserves what she gets. Lord, please forgive me." He lifted a hand toward Heaven.

"That doesn't tell me about her being an idiot, ya know, based on my definition and all," she said nonchalantly, focusing on the star-filled sky.

"I thought she liked me. I almost lost myself with her—ya know—I thought she loved me and me her." Raddix went radio silent, and Lily patiently waited for him to continue.

She worked hard not to think of Raddix *with* Selena. Was that irrational jealousy in her stomach?

"She dated me so she could get in with the quarterback. Have you heard of Dixon Bradley, quarterback for the Hawks?"

"Yeah," her voice rose with excitement.

Raddix winced. "Selena had that same desire for him, too."

Lily rolled over on her stomach, resting her chin in her palms. "Raddix, it's exciting that you played ball with a pro football player, but I don't long for Dixon Bradley."

"That's easy to say when you don't have a choice."

"Are you saying I could choose you?" Lily swallowed the lump of fear lodged in her throat, surprised at her boldness.

Fear his answer would still be no. Fear he'd say yes, and she'd put him in danger if her past ever caught up with her. She couldn't win this one.

He rolled on his side, tucked a piece of hair behind her ear, and brushed his knuckles down her cheek but ignored her question.

"You are so beautiful inside and out, Lily." Raddix's husky voice shot adrenaline through her veins.

She tucked her chin to her chest. He gently lifted it with his thumb and forefinger, searching her face until their eyes met. His sweet chocolate eyes looked at her differently this time. Was it possible he could have feelings for her? Feelings he couldn't or wouldn't ignore?

"I want to kiss you so badly, Lily." Raddix cupped her cheek, but the rest of his body stayed in his own space.

Me too! Lily broke eye contact first. "Raddix, I'm not sure your dating rules make for a great outcome. If you gave me what I think will be an out-of-this-world kiss, that would complicate things for both of us."

"Will you look at me?"

Lily slowly complied, her heart hitching the moment their gazes connected. "I'm sorry if I made things difficult, but before I apologize for too much or you tempt me any more than you already are, I need to hear more of your story to see what would complicate things."

A pang of disappointment hit Lily. She couldn't tell anyone. What if they led her past right to her new front steps? Lily knew her illogical fear and embarrassment of having a stalker was irrational, but she didn't want to share just yet.

When Raddix's phone vibrated, she got her out. His brows creased together when he read the text. "Sorry to cut this short, but Damon thinks the thieves from the other ranch are here. Come on, I'll get you to your car so you can get out of here."

"Wait. what about you?"

"I'll be good. This is what I do. Come on." Raddix held out his hand and pulled Lily to her feet. "We can talk about our next outing when I see you again."

While driving home, Lily analyzed his wording: *Our next outing*, not our third and final date. Was that significant, or was he just preoccupied with the potential danger on the ranch? Either way, she needed to figure out how to forget about Raddix Lawrence before something happened that they couldn't come back from.

Chapter 12

I t was one of Montana's hot summer days. It had to be ninety degrees or close to it. Fortunately, the humidity was low, but Raddix had shed his shirt hours ago.

"Dad, we promised Emmanuel he could brand with us the next time, so maybe we should save these last few for tomorrow. He won't feel like helping us today."

"I don't think one day will matter with the way he's feeling, and we really have to brand these babies." Raddix knew his dad was right, but he still hated to disappoint the little man.

"I hope that little guy is okay." Sean paused, pulling on the hem of his shirt to let air in. Raddix never liked to see his dad's back, so it made it easy since his dad didn't like revealing his scars—the inside ones or the outside ones—to anyone.

"Lily said she got answers the same day," Raddix declared, putting the rod iron tool in a bucket of water to cool.

"There's nothing worse than having a child suffering." Sean stared off into the distance.

"Dad?"

He waved a dismissive hand at Raddix. "I'm fine. Looks like we have company," Sean pointed toward the roadway.

"Howdy, gentlemen, how's it going this morning?" Sheriff McDugal strolled up, placing his hands on his hips, greeting the men.

Raddix shook the man's hand. "It's going. How'd you make out with the leads we gave you?"

"Well," the sheriff, a couple of years younger than Raddix, crossed his arms over his chest. "Not very good. If I were to guess, the incidents aren't related."

"How do you figure?" Sean asked curiously.

"Well, at the Radcliffe's ranch, they stole all the cows at once and had minimal damage, ironically. Here, you have damage that gets increasingly worse—first posts, then wire ripped off, now setting small fires to your fields—yet no other ranches are having any problems, and they haven't stolen any of your cattle. It seems like you've been targeted for another reason."

Raddix couldn't imagine anyone who'd want to hurt him or anyone else on Big L' Ranch. They were generous and kind.

"Besides, Myrtle said she saw a person, singular, coming from the woods the night in question."

"Those ladies are everywhere, aren't they?"

"If you only knew." The sheriff shook his head, and the pink hue on his cheeks told Raddix that the Troublesome Trio had something on the good 'ol boy.

"When did you notice the first damage?" the sheriff interrupted Raddix's thoughts.

He looked at his dad, trying to recall. "Gerard-err, Sheriff, I guess it was around the beginning of summer."

Though they went to high school together, he felt bad calling the man by his first name when he was on a call.

"No, wait," Sean interjected. "It was a week or so after the auction. All the married guys blamed us single ones for being gone, so you, Damon, and I fixed up the post on the east corner near the gravesite."

His dad was referring to his mother's grave and Amelia's parents: Uncle Jack and Aunt Marilyn. He never went there much. It was agony thinking about being alone. He could never imagine having his dad's pain. The love of his life died, and his dad became a quarter of a man. Though Raddix and his dad got along fine now, he missed his dad growing up.

"How many incidents had you had before you called the police?" The sheriff lifted his hat and wiped his forehead.

"I don't know three or four, but none like this one. It was like a warning, but I don't know for what," Raddix admitted.

"You didn't tell anyone about what we found, did you?"

"No, Sheriff. Only you, my dad, and I know about that."

"Good, don't tell anyone. That will be our key to catching this group."

Raddix exited the barn just as Quinton pulled into the driveway. The two front doors and one of the back doors opened simultaneously, and Raddix's eyes fixated on the back door. Lily had ridden with them early this morning for Emmanuel's procedures.

Her eyes met his, but she forced a smile. *Oh, no, that can't be good.* Quinton pulled Emmanuel from the back seat, and the little guy plopped his head on Quinton's shoulder.

Raddix ran over to greet them. He hated to ask, seeing how Amelia's eyes were red-rimmed. It must be bad news. "How'd you make out?"

"Emmanuel has Crohn's Disease." Quinton choked out.

"I have what?" Emmanuel's head shot up and plopped back down. "What's going on? What happened to me?"

Amelia's lips formed a straight line. "He's still groggy from the anesthesia. It only took about twenty minutes after he woke for the anesthesiologist to let us take him out, saying that a new setting would be best for him and everyone involved. Let's just say Quinton got kicked in the face."

Quinton interrupted, "Amelia took the brunt of it. I'm sure she'll be bruised tomorrow, but at least we know what to expect the next time."

Quinton cut her off, probably because he didn't want to relive it either. Raddix knew how much Quinton loved his wife.

Next time?

"We're going to head in and get Emmanuel situated, Come on, Sweetheart." Quinton tilted his head toward the house.

Raddix had been studying Lily, and he noticed her flinch when Quinton called Amelia sweetheart. Raddix had to get to the bottom of whatever the psychologist didn't want to talk about . . . pretty ironic if you asked him.

"Thank you for all you did today, Lily. You can fill Raddix in; I don't have the energy to talk about it anymore today." She turned back. "We'll see you tomorrow for dinner, right?"

"Definitely. Thank you for the advance notice so I can bring dessert."

"I love dessert," Emmanuel called out.

"I know, buddy. I'm making it especially for you, but we have to share, okay?"

"Mmm-hmm." The little guy was so out of it that Raddix's heart bled for him.

Lily smiled and waved at Amelia as she and Quinton whisked Emmanuel off to rest. "He was such a trooper today."

"Sounds like he was practicing for a MMA match." Raddix's nonchalance and deep, nervous chuckle gave him exactly what he wanted—a smile on Lily's face.

"It wasn't funny then, but maybe everyone will laugh later."

He was super sweet and funny at first. They premedicated him before the anesthesia, warning us that he would probably wake up harder than without it. He'd wanted to keep getting up once he'd realized his head was heavy—he could barely lift it off the pillow. Amelia wouldn't let him, of course. He yelled as loud as he could, "I'm not trying to run away!" The entire staff cracked up."

"That's Emmanuel."

"It was when he woke up when everything went haywire." Empathy etched her face. "He was yelling, didn't know where he was, what they did to him. He just wanted to go home, and when Quinton told him to get up so we could, he leaned real close to the edge toward his dad and said, 'I can't, you idiot.' Then came the kicking and more yelling."

"Wow." Raddix cracked his knuckles before crossing his arms over his chest.

"You're going to have arthritis before you're forty," Lily pointed to his hands.

"Arthritis. Nah, I'm almost there and don't have any signs yet."

The front door opened, and Alex and Allie strolled toward them. He didn't want to deal with either of them right now, but there wasn't a way out of it. He'd have to introduce them to Lily or risk being harassed later. They'd become even more unbearable since Amelia put a fire under them with the silage. Since they'd returned from their vacation, something seemed off with them, but Raddix couldn't quite put his finger on it. The one thing he was sure about was that Alex didn't resemble anything of his parents. Jeff and Katy were another set of parents for Raddix while growing up, and they were the best.

"Hi, Raddix." Allie stopped right between him and Lily. Allie was the gossip on the ranch, and her husband always stuck up for her. Raddix didn't mean to judge since he didn't have a wife or a girlfriend, so he didn't have a clue what he would do if his wife was that annoying. Hopefully, he'd choose better to begin with or not at all, which was the road he was headed down.

Lily introduced herself while he was lost in his thoughts, ones that had inevitably led to her.

"Raddix, are you going to give up your three strikes and your out dating rule? This one seems like a keeper." Axel really irritated him. He had to be adopted. Along with Uncle Jack, Jeff was the best father figure to him when his dad couldn't be there for him. How had Axel turned out so different?

"Time will tell." Her slackened jaw and blushed cheeks told him a lot. Maybe, just maybe, he could forget his rule for Lily.

Chapter 13

Excitement soared through Lily all day. It could have been the coffee she drank repeatedly since she hadn't slept in almost twenty hours. But, if she were to guess, the thrill rushing through her aorta had more to do with having dinner at Big L' Ranch today.

She didn't seem to be the only one excited either. When she'd walked to the diner for her latest cup of coffee, The Troublesome Trio had cornered her. Not in an I'm-going-to-kill-you way, but it had been scary nonetheless.

"Lily, dear, how are you doing?" Hazel shrieked from across the room.

"I'm fine, and you?" Lily usually held her head up proudly and pulled her hair away from her face. Right now, she was thankful for it being down, so she could hide.

Lily knew she could get out of there without any more attention if it was only Hazel. She was usually the more reserved of the group.

"We're all good," Doris said, pulling Mrytle along like it was an Olympic sport. If Lily had to guess, Doris didn't want to miss a thing. That woman's voice carried as if she spoke through a bullhorn.

Everyone noticed her now.

Doris was always fashionable and reminded Lily of Rose Nylan, the Golden Girl played by Betty White, with regards to perfectly done-up hair that didn't move; it bounced. The woman's clothing and personality were more in line with Blanche, the provocative Golden Girl.

Then there's Myrtle, who didn't remind her of either of the other Golden Girls. She wore outlandish clothing most of the time and spent her free time (which seemed to be all day, every day) scheming or intruding into people's lives. Her teal skin-tight leggings with black, salmon, yellow, and orange shaped blobs plastered on each leg by themselves were a fashion no-no for anyone, but definitely worse on the septuagenarian, despite her thin frame.

A little out of breath, Mrytle said, "I heard that sexy cowboy saved you from a car trying to run you down."

"That might be a bit of an exaggeration about all accounts *except for the sexy cowboy part*, but yeah, I made it out alive."

Hazel got close and whispered, "He's definitely a keeper."

"He sure is, but he's not interested in being kept," Lily chuckled. She wasn't sure why she was whispering, but it sure beat having everyone staring at her.

"Crazier things have happened in this town. Give him time, he'll come around." Myrtle nudged Doris with her elbow, sending her winks and smiles.

"I have to get back. Don't you ladies start or cause any trouble today. I've heard all about you," Lily giggled.

"We won't," they answered in unison.

They are definitely up to something. I can see it in their eyes.

Her ringtone pulled her from her high as she walked back to her apartment. Disappointment clutched her heart. She took a deep breath and let it out slowly before answering the call.

"Hi, Selena. How are you?"

"Not good. Can I please come over and talk? Of course, I'll pay you for a drop-in session."

Lily hated to turn anyone away who sounded as distraught as Selena did. Sometimes, she had to manage her own mental health, but today, she wanted to help Selena.

"Please, I just need to talk something through with you, and even if it doesn't take the whole hour, I'll still pay you for that."

Looking at her watch, Lily figured she could get ready now and leave as soon as Selena left. "Okay, but I only have an hour."

A loud bang outside caused Lily to jump. It was startling how rapidly she could be pulled into a state of fear.

Absurd.

She repeated to herself, "Calm down, calm down," as she hurried into her bedroom. Scanning through the clothes in her closet, she pulled out a sleek tank top and threw it on her bed. Rummaging through her bureau drawers, she found her favorite pair of jean shorts and tossed them on the bed, too.

"Grand Central Station," she hissed out loud when a text interrupted her ability to get ready.

That frustration quickly turned to pleasure when she saw that, for the first time ever, Raddix had texted her. She didn't even know what he wanted. Did it matter? Nope! He could have texted to tell her his grocery list or accidentally sent her a text meant for someone else, and she would have been happy to see his name across her phone.

Oh, dear. She was in Big. Trouble. One, the looming threat of harm reaching Raddix made her nauseous. She'd never forgive herself if anything bad happened to him. Second, Raddix hadn't dated a woman more than three times, and she'd already had two. Yuck!

> **Hey, Lily. It's Raddix. I have to head into town shortly. Just wondering if you'd like a ride to the ranch?**

Three dots kept appearing and disappearing like he was trying to say something else and didn't know how or wasn't sure how Lily would respond to whatever he had to say.

After a minute of cell phone silence, Lily responded.

> **Sure, if it's not any trouble.**

> **None at all.**

His response came in immediately.

> **Oh, wait.**

A mischievous smile formed on Lily's face as she looked at her phone, wondering if Raddix was gripping his phone as tightly as she had been minutes ago.

> **This doesn't count as our third date, right? I may have to decline the ride if so *wink emoji***

The *Ha Ha* reaction pinged on her phone next to her text. Then, the three dots appeared again.

> **No, this definitely doesn't count as our third date.**

Her smile reached her ears, and her heart soared far beyond the universe. Then her doorbell rang, bringing her back to reality. She better warn him.

> **I have a one-hour session right now, then I should be ready to go.**

> **Sounds good. See ya soon.**

Lily paused with her hand on the doorknob. She blew out a breath and whipped open the door. "Hi, Selena. How are you?"

"Just devastated." She pushed her way past Lily.

"Please, come in," she whispered under her breath as she shut the door.

The small room she used as her office had two chairs facing each other and one small stand beside the patient's chair for belongings.

"How can I help you?"

"This is more about me helping you. I was at Big L' Ranch today, picking up my dad's order, and started talking with Raddix about getting back together. He told me maybe, but he had to take care of something tonight first."

"Interesting. Did he give you any indication what that was?"

"I'm sorry to tell you this, but" Selena's statue features told Lily that this woman didn't have an empathetic bone in her body, at least not at the moment. "He needs to break things off with you, but he felt bad about the accident and wanted to make sure you were okay. You know, not still shaken up."

Had news really traveled that fast? They hadn't called the sheriff about the car. Did someone from the ranch talk? "Break things off with me? We aren't anything, so I think you might have misunderstood something along the way. As far as the car, I haven't thought about it since that moment. I think it was just someone driving fast down an unmonitored road. No harm, no foul."

"Maybe I did misunderstand, but I thought it was important for you to know." Selena's saccharine sweet tone, lined with a bit of venom, sent icy chills down Lily's back. She didn't need any more complications in her life.

"Well, I appreciate the heads up, but you don't have to worry about stepping on my toes. We went out a couple of times, and from what I gather, he doesn't date a woman more than three times, so I'd say you're good to go."

"Yeah," her tone quickly changed to a spirited Barbie wanna-be. "That's because I broke his heart, but I'm sure that rule won't apply to me."

An awkward silence stretched her session time. "If you're better, I think we can be done here." Lily kept her tone professional, though she wanted to kick this woman out of her space.

"Yeah, I feel much better."

I bet you do. Lily kept a fake smile plastered on her face despite her unkind thoughts.

The moment Selena left, she texted Raddix.

> **Hey, I'm good with a ride. I can drive myself, thanks for the invitation though.**

Lily didn't see the point in getting any closer to Raddix; she already knew he was great. If she were being honest, she'd have to admit that her attraction ran deep. If there hadn't been the threat of death looming over his head, she would have pursued him earlier, ignoring his three-date rule. Instead, this seemed like the perfect time to let him go.

Chapter 14

R addix's blood raced when Lily texted him again.

What changed?

I had a visit from someone who is clearly wrapped up in you, or you are in her, IDK, and I don't want to get in the middle of that.

Excuse me?

He was still ten minutes away. Who could have turned Lily against him?

After a brief mental search, he knew right away. He clenched his jaw, causing his eye to twitch; not a normal occurrence for him, but the she-devil brought out the worst in everyone around her, and he refused to let her get to his sweet Lily.

What?! She's not *his* Lily, but maybe she could be. He'd spent a lot of time thinking about having a family of his own, making him intimately aware of how much he wanted that with Lily.

Lemme guess, Selena paid you a visit?

Another minute passed of silence on her end. He sent one final text.

I'm almost there. We'll talk about it when I get there. Voice dictation through the speaker is more trouble than it's worth.

Besides, he wanted to see her. If this interaction was anything like his dream last night, he'd be a happy man.

Chapter 15

Suck it up, buttercup. Raddix was never yours to begin with. Lily had a difficult time believing Selena based on what Raddix had told her on their dates, and the more she got to know Raddix, he hadn't seemed like the type to lie. Three quick raps on her door pulled Lily from her musing.

Before opening the door, she coached herself. *Be strong; don't fall for anything he has to say.* A slight breeze carried a yummy scent into her house when she opened the door. She'd know it anywhere—coconut mahogany—her favorite. Could he have known that? She didn't think so. Another point in his favor.

"Come on in." Lily stepped back and swept her hand toward her entryway.

"Thank you." Raddix took off his hat and clutched it in one hand at his waist. Lily had never seen him look so nervous, or was this his guilty look?

"So, I can't really divulge what I learned because it was in a session, and that's all confidential, so I don't really have anything to say," Lily declared.

Raddix took a step closer. Her heart fluttered at his nearness. His presence and alluring scent overpowered her, breaking down her defenses.

"Since you can't tell me anything, let me see if I can guess what happened. Selena, the wicked witch of Central Montana, came here and trashed me."

Lily shook her head.

"She came here and . . ." he tried again. Raddix's gaze flitted around the room, making Lily think that he didn't have a clue what the woman would say if she hadn't said something mean.

"Let's just say I think keeping our distance is best. I have it under good authority that you are spoken for, or at the very least, someone is vying for you, and I am just in the way."

A big, boisterous laughter caught Lily off guard. "Woman, I am not spoken for by anyone. If I ever let a woman capture me, it wouldn't be a prairie rattlesnake like Selena Whittaker."

Lily's heart raced first when he called her Woman. The huskiness of his deep, gravelly voice appealed to her. Coupled with the longing look in his eyes when he fixed his gaze on her, Lily was in danger of believing anything he said.

Raddix moved even closer, setting his hat on the counter and running his hand through his hair right before he rested his palms on her shoulders. "You're looking a little green. Are you okay, Darlin'?"

Darlin"? Who did he think he was? Had she really given off jealousy vibes?

"I'm fine, Dumplin'," she mocked him with a nickname, causing him to tip his head back and laugh, exposing his thick neck and the slightest movement of his Adam's apple.

His laughter was melodious, like Mozart or Tchaikovsky, and she wanted to hear more of it.

"Let me make myself crystal clear," Raddix slowly backed Lily into the counter and rested his hands on either side of her, leaning even closer until their breath mingled. "I am not, nor will I ever be, interested in Selena. But . . ." he straightened to full height, "I think you're cute when you're jealous."

Lily playfully swatted his bicep. "I am not jealous." She played up a shocked expression regarding his buffness. "Oh, my, my mister, I only date a woman three times before breaking her heart." Lily squeezed his arm. "Cowboy, what strong muscles you have." Lily then used both hands to squeeze his bicep, which was a bit of a challenge since he flexed, bulging out even more.

"Are we good to go?" Raddix created space between them by moving toward the door.

"No. I have to change, and I have to wrap the pies." Lily's heart gushed when he gave her a once over.

"You look fine to me."

She'd never stop blushing if he kept saying things like that to her. Then a thought came to her. She'd accused him of being a flirt, but she started believing it was more than that.

"I made a banana cream pie, but I think it smells spoiled. Are you good at telling?"

"You think I would be because I milk cows for a living?" Raddix pretended to be offended.

"Well, yeah, I guess when you put it that way, I was right to think you could help with this one."

Lily lifted the pie toward Raddix. As he bent closer, Lily pushed the container into his face and swirled it around. As her hand dropped the tin pie holder, she roared with the hardest belly laugh she'd produced in a long time.

Raddix stuck his tongue out, tasting the pie filling. "At least it tastes good, but what will you do about bringing a dessert?"

Tossing her thumb over her shoulder, she quipped, "Oh, that's no problem. I made more." His eyes locked on her, and she saw his slow-producing Grinch-like smile. She was in trouble. He'd get his vengeance for her little stunt. "You planned this?"

He grabbed her hips. "Is this okay?"

He'd asked her this on their second date, right before he was about to kiss her, or so she thought. Erratic breathing filled her chest. She clutched onto his bicep and opposite shoulder and whimpered, "Yeah." Finally, they were going to have their first kiss.

"It's a shame that you made such a great pie and didn't get to try any of it."

Before she could protest, he rubbed his pie-plastered face along her cheek and the other cheek, smearing the fruity goodness on her shoulder and the front of her shirt. She wouldn't complain. Pie covered his shirt, so he'd definitely gotten the worst of it.

Besides, what girl in her right mind would complain about a handsome cowboy nuzzling up to her face? Their lips had almost grazed one another, and her heart hitched with anticipation before he quickly wiped his cheek down her neck.

"You made me a mess," Lily squealed, still laughing.

"Not possible. Do you want me to clean you up?"

Stunned, she froze in place, now engaged in the most intense staring contest she'd ever had with anyone. *Was he serious right now?*

"I'm too big of a mess," she wasn't necessarily talking about the current pie situation.

"I'd love to try if you let me." he pulled the dishtowel off the counter and wiped most of the pie off his face in one swoop.

WHAT! Holy cow. Her heart took flight. He'd just won the Swoony Statement of the Year!

She still hadn't answered him, but he crept closer to her until his hands cupped her elbows, sending ripples of delight down her arms. His dreamy eyes never left hers. Raddix's chest was heaving, matching the pace and rhythm of Lily's. *This can't be happening. I've been warned.*

"Lily," his deep, masculine voice shot electricity down her spine. Since when had a man's voice affected her like this?

Never!

"I tried to avoid this, but you are so dang appealing; I don't want to anymore." He paused. Hopefully, he wasn't waiting for her to respond because her mind had turned to mush. The only thing working was her heart, which kept repeating, "Kiss me." Until eventually her mouth must have followed suit since he smiled and moved closer still.

For the first time since moving here, she didn't think about consequences, she let herself go and enjoyed the moment with Raddix who was closing in even more.

Chapter 16

"With pleasure." Raddix didn't hesitate. Running his hands up her arms, he gripped her shoulders, pulling her closer. His lips met hers with soft, gentle brushes. Gliding his hands up her neck, he tenderly tilted her head, deepening the kiss. The sweet mix of banana cream pie on her tongue and what seemed to be coconut lip gloss, coupled with the little moan Lily let escape her throat as she melted into his arms, sent a surge of electricity through his body.

Weaving his fingers through her hair, he released the pent-up passion he had held since their first date. She matched him kiss for kiss, just about undoing him when her hands traveled over the bare skin on his neck up into his hair, where she massaged his scalp, sending tingles down his spine.

Releasing a low growl, he trailed kisses down her cheek and neck, pausing briefly to nip at her earlobe. Not the smartest thing, he realized, when the back of her earring poked him in the lip, but he didn't care at the moment. She tilted to the side, giving him more access to her neck. "You are dangerous, woman," he said, wrapping his arms tightly around her waist, nearly lifting her completely off the floor.

When she giggled, he felt the vibration from her in his chest on his own, and it shot right to his toes! "You're pretty dangerous yourself, Cowboy."

"Raddix?" Her soft, sweet voice tugged at his heart. He'd move heaven and Earth to please her when she spoke to him like that. "What are we doing?"

"Dang, If you have to ask, Darlin', I must be rustier than I thought."

She playfully slapped him on the shoulder as he swayed her back and forth in his arms.

"Oh, if that's you being rusty, I could never handle you at peak performance," Lily's admission made her blush. "I mean, you don't date a woman more than three times, and I'm not free to date."

"For people who don't or can't date, we can certainly make out well together."

"Stop joking for just a second. I'm being serious." Lily rested her forehead on his shoulder.

He loved the feel of her in his arms, but Raddix needed more at the moment. Keeping one arm around her waist, he pulled her back slightly, lifting her chin so their eyes met. "What do you want from me, Darlin'?"

His breathing picked up, and his whole body felt like pins and needles when she didn't respond. Maybe this was a bad idea. He still didn't know why she couldn't date. She hadn't told him yet, but depending on how she answered, he was ready to put a moratorium on his three-date rule. Not that he was ready to profess his love or walk down the aisle in any conceivable way. Still, he could adopt a new rule, right? Perhaps it should be that he only dates Lily. Yes, that sounded like a solid rule, but her silence was unnerving.

"It's not a trick question. I can tell your mind is racing; just tell me," Raddix urged, trying to calm his nerves. He needed to know what she was thinking either way.

His phone rang. "Ignore it," Raddix muttered, wanting her to answer his question. When his phone rang again, Lily urged, "You need to get that. Something could be wrong."

He pulled away. "Ugh, sorry." Raddix let out a frustrated sigh, apologizing for the interruption and her pie-lathered shirt. "It's Amelia."

"This better be—"

"—Raddix, you need to get back here. There's more damage."

"I'm on my way."

Chapter 17

Dinner at the ranch had become her new favorite pastime. Emmanuel loved the homemade pie that Lily promised to make him again. She spent most of her time talking with him as he expressed his feelings about his new diagnosis.

"How are you doing, my friend?" Lily asked in a neutral tone as she sat on the couch and Emmanuel sat on his indoor trampoline.

"Not so great, my friend," Emmanuel replied matching her inflection, making Lily smile at how personable he was. This little guy was the cutest human she'd ever had the pleasure of knowing.

"I can't have anything I like, and it's not fair. Everyone else is going to eat all that stuff right in front of my face, and that's just mean."

Lily offered him a sympathetic smile.

"What's that look mean?" Emmanuel asked.

"It means I feel bad for you. I've been where you are, and I know how upsetting it is. I'm going to tell you something, and you won't believe me right now, but I'm proof it's true." She paused, making sure he was listening. "Things will get better, you'll figure out the food stuff, and then the most important part is getting into remission."

"I can't have Cheetos or bagels—"

"—Yes, you can." Lily didn't like interrupting her patients because that's how she learned so much about them, but this was the fifth time she'd heard this exact rant from him tonight, and she wanted to take his fears away."

"How?"

"Emmanuel, you're lucky because Carolyn and Cash make your food from scratch. I already talked with them for you and shared everything I knew about Crohn's Disease and what to stay away from. There are some preservatives in foods that people don't even realize are bad for them, but if I learned this, so can you."

"Really?"

"You already have homemade bagels, those are fine. Carolyn said she'd try to make homemade cream cheese because there isn't a cream cheese on this planet without some type of gum in it. Trust me, I've looked. She promised to let me try it when she perfects it. That has not been my specialty." She crinkled up her nose and shook her head, getting the slightest quiver of Emmanuel's lips.

Anything you see in the store you can make in your house, but you'll do it without all the chemicals. Living here, you have the greatest food in the world—fresh, without chemicals. Don't even get me started on how lucky you are to have Cash and Carolyn."

"It won't taste the same," he argued.

"Somethings won't you're right." She thought of her attempt at cream cheese. "But somethings will be even better."

Lily saw that mischievous look in his eyes as he tilted his head and brushed his fingers together rapidly. "What about my Cheetos, huh? You said I could have those."

"Once you're in remission, you can have treats every now and then." Lily leaned really close and whispered, "Do you want to know something, though? You probably won't want those toxic foods by that time because your body is going to thank you for eating this way."

"Why are we whispering," Emmanuel asked, again causing Lily to feel blessed just being in the same room as him.

"Hey," Raddix leaned on the door frame, capturing Emmanuel's attention. "Anyone want to go set up some traps with me?" Lily looked, and she shouldn't have. Men must take a course that tells them to put on a hat and lean against something to get their woman interested. Not that she was *his* woman. He could have any woman, especially in that pose.

"Yeah!" Emmanuel jumped up and shot his fist into the air.

"How about you, Darlin'?" Raddix pinned his eyes on her. Lily swallowed hard, trying to recapture her thought process. She looked at her watch.

One bad thing about working remotely is that work could happen at all hours if the therapist was willing. She had a pretentious millionaire who could only meet at nine-thirty at night, Lily's time. Fortunately, it was only once a week, but sometimes the woman had a lot to talk about, and she was always willing to pay, so Lily never refused her more time, especially since she couldn't sleep at night anyway.

"I've got a little bit of time."

"I know all this," Emmanuel said impatiently.

"Yeah, my dad gave me the bear one-oh-one talk on a trip to Lake Tahoe when I was three, so you're a little behind," she teased.

"I've had more experience dealing—"

"—Clearly," Lily interrupted.

"Are you insinuating that I'm old?" The corners of Raddix's mouth lifted.

"I wasn't insinuating it. Just calling it like I see it." She needled him right back.

"You're both old! Can we get to setting the traps?" Emmanuel never held back. She loved that about him.

Lily studied his sun-kissed face while he gave her the basic rules of what to do if she met a bear up close. The sun was setting quickly, becoming her primary focus.

"Rule number one: stay calm; have no fear. Rule number two: always move sideways, never backward." Lily bit the inside of her cheek, preventing herself from smiling at his animated movement. "Rule number three: stand beside a tree or something large to make your sweet, little frame appear larger."

Her eyebrows raised, questioning his comment, and the look on Raddix's face blasted her insides with excitement. But he rambled on, void of any further looks, making her wonder if those earth-shattering kisses back at her apartment meant as much to him as they did her.

Who was she kidding? She couldn't date him given her current dilemma. Lily wouldn't put him in danger. If she were being honest with herself though, it was pretty irrational that a stalker would follow her all the way from California. She'd covered her tracks pretty well, though she might be biased in her thinking. With as many women as there are in California, Lily had to be a distant memory in that man's mind.

"Rule number four: don't wound it, or it will be more of a threat. And rule number five: Never, ever run!"

She'd heard this all before. Between Raddix's alarming tone and steeled eyes, she was scared. Fear had already swindled her from a normal life. Her irrational thoughts filled her mind regularly. Now, it was seeping into other areas of her life.

She squeezed her arms around her midsection to soothe her shaking insides. Nope, that hadn't helped. If she met a bear in the wild, would she be able to follow these rules? She'd run away from the bear in California. Was he chasing her? *No, that's not logical!* She rebuked herself as Raddix stared at her. Had she wounded him, making him more dangerous? Was the demented stalker trying to hunt her down and take care of her? *Dear God, please, no!*

"Thanks for the lesson, but now I don't think I have time to help with the fun stuff. I should get going to prepare for my next client."

He looked at his watch. "I thought you had more time?" His voice seemed to have an edge. Was he mad? A flicker of his eyes revealed more disappointment than anger. That was a relief.

"Y-yeah, I need to prepare, and I don't want it to get too dark. I'll see if Amelia can take me home so you and Emmanuel can stop these bad guys and avoid any bears while you're setting human traps." She held out her fist for Emmanuel to fist-bump him and headed back to the main house.

"Lily, remember, the most important thing in life, bear or otherwise—never run."

Tears pricked her eyes. She could have thrown those words right back at him. One minute, he'd been kind and sweet. Then, the next moment, he'd given her the three-dates-only rule, and now he was laying it on thick again. Lily knew she'd be deflecting if she said anything, but she wasn't wrong about his behavior. Nor was he wrong about hers.

"Duly noted." Lily forced a partial smile before leaving.

Chapter 18

The last time he'd felt this way was when . . . never! This unfamiliar feeling had his gut turning, his chest spasming, and his mind racing. Lily had him doubting himself and his way of life.

"Man, what's wrong with you today?" Quinton had returned from the west side of the ranch with Duncan. It was interesting that all the damage happened on the east side. Why wouldn't the group spread it around? Why hadn't they done any stakeouts to catch the culprits?

"All clear on the west side, not a scratch insight. You know. I spoke with Amelia about the two hundred-plus acres she got from Mr. Banks."

"Yeah, what about it?" Based on another assessment this morning, the house needs a lot of work. We think you should have that property and make it your own."

Raddix froze, brush in hand, just above Blaze's back. Blaze was their best horse for rotating the herd. "I don't know what to say."

"Well, don't say anything yet. Amelia wanted to be the one to tell you." Quinton shrugged before dismounting. Leading Duncan into his stall, he grabbed a brush. "Want to talk about it?"

"Not really."

"I get it."

Raddix huffed out a breath. "She's perfect. Never makes me feel like my thinking or feelings are wrong. She tells me how handsome I am. How could she not, right?"

Quinton guffawed, causing Raddix's brows to crease.

"What the problem then? Are you really going to hold yourself to a stupid rule that you didn't even set for yourself?"

"What do you mean?"

Jeff told me Alex teased you years ago that since Selena had broken your heart, you hadn't dated the same woman more than three times."

"Really?"

"Seriously, you don't remember? Raddix, why are you punishing yourself and taking on someone else's idiocy?"

Raddix smiled inward, relishing that Quinton wasn't a fan of Alex or Allie either.

"Well, that's not all."

Quinton circled his wrist quickly, motioning for Raddix to pick up the story's pace.

"She's petrified of something. She won't accept roses and can't stand hearing the word sweetheart and not just from me. When you called Amelia sweetheart one day, she cringed. I don't know what's going on with that, and unless she tells me, I can't move forward."

"Just ask her."

"I have. We've been interrupted every time."

Quinton shook his head. "If I could break through Amelia's walls, you can surely discover what Lily is hiding. The bigger question is, do you care enough? It seems like the answer is yes, which leads to another question. When will you let her know in no uncertain terms that you're ready for a relationship with her?"

"I didn't say that," Raddix's voice boomed.

"You didn't have to. The way you just responded told me everything I needed to know."

"I don't want to be hurt," Raddix said. He hated being vulnerable with anyone, and if anyone other than Quinton (or Damon if he wasn't off picking up a new mustang) had stood in front of him, he wouldn't have revealed anything.

Quinton grinned. "I hate to be the bearer of bad news, but if you and Lily start a relationship, you will be hurt more than you'd think. The ones closest to us hurt us the most because we care about them."

"I thought Lily was the psychologist. When did you turn into Sigmund Freud?

"I'm not a psychologist, but I've been hurt enough to know." Quinton continued to brush Duncan after Raddix put his brush away and patted Blaze's side.

I am so enthralled with her that I can't sleep well at night. During the day, it's worse. My mind races, thinking about her. I wonder what . . .well, I wonder a lot."

Quinton held up his hand. "I got it. Listen, you have to tell her and risk rejection, or you'll never know what happiness feels like."

Raddix knew what he needed to do—pray nonstop. He trusted the Lord and would follow him anywhere, even if that led him to heartache.

Chapter 19

"Hey, Lily, Emmanuel is beyond excited to see you," Amelia moved in closer and whispered, "I think someone else is just as excited, but he's out in the field right now."

Lily avoided looking at Amelia, hoping Emmanuel would appear any second. Admitting how much she enjoyed hearing that made her more vulnerable than she liked.

"He's a good man," Amelia's voice softened.

That went without saying as far as Lily was concerned. He'd even hinted at dismissing his dating rule for *her*. Could she ever trust him or anyone else in this sweet town with her past? More than that, would the stalker make good on his threat? She couldn't bear anything happening to Raddix.

"I know," she replied softly. "How are things going with Emmanuel?" Lily shifted the focus back to the purpose of her being there.

"Besides struggling with the things he can't eat, he still has difficulty bathing and brushing his teeth." Amelia sighed, visually exhausted.

Lily gave the woman a compassionate smile. "We can talk about that today. I'm not sure if the doctor told you, but Crohn's affects your teeth and mouth, so it's important he works to be independent with those tasks."

She watched as Emmanuel came barreling out the door barefoot, the hinges on the storm door squealing at the force he'd inflicted upon them.

"What's wrong, Buddy," Amelia's concern was evident as she moved toward Emmanuel with her arms open if he wanted her. He didn't, so she put her hands down.

"Well, Buddy, I'm hungry, and there isn't anything in this stupid house to eat."

"Do you want to take Lily to the orchard? I bet the summer fruit is ready. Alex and Allie could give you some options."

"Fruit, fruit, fruit. I'm sick of fruit," Emmanuel theatrically waved his hands about before plopping into a nearby chair.

He lifted his feet. "I don't have any shoes, and I'm not walking on the grass without my shoes."

"Emmanuel, why did you come out of the house without shoes if you knew it bothered you?" Lily wondered aloud.

"Cuz I had to come here because *you're here.*"

"Tone." Amelia steeled her voice.

Lily waved it off, knowing that would be something to work with him on, but right now, it was probably not the time. Emmanuel was a hot mess, and they needed to solve one of his problems at a time.

"Do you want to talk today, Emmanuel, or are you in a bad place."

He stared off. If Lily hadn't already started to understand his mannerisms, she might have thought he was ignoring her, but she knew he was thinking. Amelia's silence revealed her understanding, too.

A bang behind her grabbed her attention. Her breath hitched. She snapped her slackened jaw shut before anyone noticed. When she heard Amelia chuckle behind her, she knew she hadn't shut it quick enough. Oh well. She couldn't help it if she noticed a handsome, shirtless, cowboy. She thought the first time she saw him without his shirt had taken her breath away. This time, it felt more intimate. Perhaps it was the knock-your-socks-off kiss they'd since shared or the streaks of dirt on his forearms. He worked hard, and she'd seen it when they hung out after he'd put in a long day.

But seeing him in the middle of the day with the sun beating on him and sweat glistening on his face and chest. . .

Girrrl. Breath.

"Mom, will you please get my shoes?" Emmanuel's polite request pulled Lily back to her purpose, turning her back on the handsome cowboy so she could calm her erratic pulse.

"That was a very nice way to ask for what you want," Lily saw the slightest twitch on one corner of his mouth. She'd get him to smile sometime.

"Thank you." He crossed his foot, resting his ankle on his opposite knee.

"Man, Emmanuel, your feet are dirty." Lily's joking tone didn't erase the fact, but she didn't want him to shut down. Maybe they could talk about his reason for not liking baths.

"Are they dirty like the disciples?" he quipped.

"Not quite."

Emmanuel stated flatly, "Then it's not time for a bath."

Amelia spoke up, addressing Lily. "Emmanuel said that people don't take baths in the winter because it's too cold, but now he has another excuse for not to take baths in the summer."

"Yup." Emmanuel raised a finger and tilted his head like he had the theory to end all theories. "Since I swim, I get clean and don't need a bath." He hopped up from the chair and crossed his arms over his chest. "I told them to put a bowl at the door like they did in Bible times to wash my feet."

A laugh escaped Lily's throat. She sent Amelia an apologetic look, feeling bad that she had to deal with Emmanuel's intelligence on a daily basis.

"Come on, let's go play," Emmanuel hollered, gaining the attention of the entire group of cowboys all downing water by the fence. The same group Emmanuel was leading her to now.

Lily interjected. "What is it about the bath you don't like?"

"Soap and washing my hair."

"That makes sense. Thank you for telling me. Now, your parents and I can create a plan to help you."

"Yeah, like I don't have to take a bath."

Lily enjoyed bantering with Emmanuel. Most of the time, he was like a little old man when he talked. Sometimes, however, he was so fixated on wanting things his way that it turned his bonfire of a life into a dumpster fire.

"Uncle Raddix, we're going to get some fruit because that's apparently all I can eat now," the sarcasm dripped from Emmanuel's tongue. "Can you come with us?"

Please say no or yes. Lily's conflicting emotions were getting the best of her and a hollow feeling developed in her stomach.

"Sorry, we've just taken a break. This heat is murder today." Raddix left his gang hovering by the fence to join Emmanuel and Lily.

"What's that mean, murder?"

"It means it's really hot," Raddix explained. "Wouldn't you say so, Doc?' His knowing smile irritated Lily.

More disturbing was her inability to speak, like she had a baseball-sized lump clogging her throat. Hot was definitely the right word to use.

"Mmm-hmm," she finally produced sounds, causing him to laugh out right. Simultaneously, he pulled off his hat and wiped his brow.

"I'll take that." Her voice finally broke through as she snatched his hat, but was met with numerous ch*eers* and whistles that she didn't understand.

Just as she was about to put Raddix's hat on her head, Emmanuel hollered, "Don't!"

Startled, Lily froze. "Why not?"

"I don't know. My dad said he'd tell me when I'm older." That got a laugh out of everyone except for her and Emmanuel. "All I know," he took a hard breath in, "Dad said a cowboy has to be the one to put his hat on his girl's head. If the girl takes it and puts it on her own head," Emmanuel shook his. "My dad said she's wild and stay away."

Lily gasped, understanding enough. Her shock caused her to drop his hat. "I'm so sorry," she bent over to get it and handed it back to him, holding it between her thumb and forefinger. "Here, please take it."

He moved painstakingly slow with a smile that put the Joker to shame. "I'll drop it again. I'm sure that means something crazy, too, huh?"

"Thank you." Raddix took his hat back, intentionally grabbing her wrist before she could turn away. He kissed the inside of her palm. "How about our third date? Are you available tonight?"

Her brain was a chaotic mess right now, but there was no way she'd turn down a date with this man. "Sure."

"I'll pick you up at seven, okay? I'll have Carolyn pack our dinner for a picnic."

"Come on, Lily, let's go to the orchard. I'm hungry. Sorry, Uncle Raddix, you must book your own time with her. She's mine right now."

"Outsmarted by a nine-year-old." Damon hollered.

Raddix didn't let go of her wrist yet. The intensity in his eyes made her shoulders sag. Could he already see what she was hiding? It sure seemed like it. She couldn't-err didn't want to ignore her feelings for Raddix anymore.

But it would take more than this handsome man, smelling like leather, hay, and hard work, to convince her to put him in danger.

"Just one more thing. I can see you in my hat very soon."

Much to her chagrin, heat settled in her cheeks. Never before had she been affected by a man like this. Sadly, she didn't see any way to express her feelings without jeopardizing his safety.

Slipping away from Raddix, Lily strolled away with Emmanuel. Against her better judgment, she looked over her shoulder and met Raddix's soft eyes as he gazed back at her. Maybe it was time to pack up and move again?

Chapter 20

"Things are about to get real," Raddix whispered aloud as he knocked on Lily's door.

Why was he so nervous? Perhaps since everyone made such a big deal about this being their third date, that heightened his awareness of the fact that he didn't want this to be their final date. He knew Quinton was right. If he didn't put himself out there, he'd never have an opportunity to be happy, and he wanted that more than ever with Lily.

When she opened the door, he knew something was off. Her red-rimmed eyes, bare feet, arms wrapped around herself in a way-too-big sweatshirt, and cut-off jean shorts caused his heart to drop. "What's wrong, Darlin'?" Raddix crossed the threshold in a frenzy, capturing her shoulders, waiting for her to say something. He pulled her close to his chest when he realized she wouldn't.

Seconds later, the wetness on his shirt had his heart racing out of control. He tried to think about the things she'd shared. She was diagnosed with Crohn's when she was twelve. She'd lost her family—father, mother, and younger brother—in a boating accident almost a year ago. She had never admitted this, but Raddix assumed that was her reason for leaving California. Lily had left all her clients behind and relocated here. *Is that all he knew?"* It seemed like he'd learned so much about her, and he had—that was the only possible explanation for the strong attraction pulling her toward him—but he couldn't think straight.

Her past. Raddix knew very little about it. Why was she keeping it from him? *How could he fix this if she didn't talk to him?*

"I don't mind you soaking my shirt and all," he teased, "but I'd like to help you, and in order to do that, Darlin', you have to talk to me."

She shook her head. "Not right now." She pulled away from him. His body rebelled at the loss of her warmth nestled against his chest. They fit together perfectly.

"I need to get changed," she ran her palms down her cheeks, wiping the remnant of tears away.

"You look perfect," his voice and eyes softer than he'd ever imagined they could be, but it was the truth. Lily was the most beautiful woman he'd ever met.

The blush on her cheeks had the blood in his veins pumping faster. If she could only see what Raddix saw . . .

"Maybe we should stay here instead of heading out," Raddix suggested.

Lily shook her head. "No, it's okay. I want to do whatever you planned."

"We can do it right here. I'll get the picnic basket from my truck. Do you want to make a spot for us to eat here?"

"Sure." Raddix winked before turning and headed for the door, only for Lily to stop him.

"Raddix." her voice sounded so vulnerable that he wanted to rush back to her and wrap her petite frame in his arms.

"Yeah."

"Thank you." It was so simple. Two words, but more than that, it was the look of admiration and lovingness that clutched his heart. At that moment, he knew he had fallen for Lily Peters.

"Anything for you." He waited a second, but she remained speechless, satisfying him that he could reach her, too.

The food was delicious. Emmanuel and Amelia had learned all of Lily's favorite foods as she helped Emmanuel settle on what he could eat. Carolyn and Cash had made all of them.

Raddix never knew that natural peanut butter with homemade strawberry jelly on homemade sourdough bread could taste so good. Simple.

In his mind, that was Lily. She was sweet and didn't present any complicated drama like the other women he'd dated, except that she was hiding her past, but once they got through that, they'd be good. Her down-to-earth mentality was her most attractive feature, which complemented her feminine curves, soft skin, and silky hair, which he'd been weaving his fingers through for the past ten minutes while she rested on his chest.

"I think I'm falling for you, Lily." Her shoulders stiffened. He sounded less confident than he felt. Maybe that was the wrong thing to say. She'd stopped crying enough to eat and laugh with him, music to his ears, but evidently, she wasn't ready for any declaration of feelings.

"Never mind. Forget I said anything." Sitting up, Lily pulled her knees toward her chest and rested her hands on her thighs. Each movement pulled her away from Raddix, and he felt the sting of each one.

"Why? Did you really mean what you said, or was it some macho thing you say to put women in a trance and suck them in?"

He hadn't expected that. Not sure if he should be angry or laugh. He tried to convey something in the middle. "So now, I'm some type of stalker who hunts women down, gets them to like me, and then what?"

Before Lily hopped up, he spied welled up tears in her eyes. *Shoot!* Now he'd done it. She looked even more upset than when he'd arrived.

Faster than her, Raddix popped to his sock-covered feet, tenderly grabbing her shoulders. "I'm not sure exactly what upset you, but I am sorry. The last thing I want to do is make you mad or sad. For the record, I'm not a stalker. I am Raddix Lawrence, all cowboy."

"It's okay. I just overreacted. Stupid female hormones," Lily waved her hand dismissively.

Raddix wasn't sure he believed her. Was she trying to scare him off? Didn't she realize he worked on a ranch with just as many women as men? He wasn't a stranger to *female hormones.*

"You have to let me in, Lily, if this is going to work."

Her eyes blackened. "If what's going to work? Isn't this the infamous third date? Aren't we done after this?"

He offered a faint smile. "I was hoping it wouldn't be, but I'm guessing we're not on the same page."

"I can't date you, no matter how badly I want to. You're probably in danger right now."

"What are you talking about?" Raddix snapped.

"Nothing. It's not your problem."

Raddix popped his knuckles quickly before crossing his arms over his chest. "It may not be my problem directly, but if it affects you, I take it as a hurdle I must clear, too." Raddix stared her down, causing her to look away first. We wanted to know everything about her, so much so that his brain hurt.

Lily opened her mouth to speak, but Raddix cut her off.

"I'm sorry for snapping at you." He hoped she heard the desperation in his voice. "I can tell you are terrified of something, and you won't tell me. How am I supposed to help you?"

Lily shook her head. "Don't worry about protecting me. Just save yourself."

"From what?" He pulled her close and ran a hand down her smooth hair before resting it on her shoulders.

"Back in California—"

A text interrupted their moment, and then another and another. Based on the successive text alerts, he knew it was the sheriff. Normal people just texted one sentence or thought, not him. Now, he might never know what was going on with Lily. Raddix released a frustrated growl.

He would have ignored it, but he'd been getting updates from McDugal all day. The man was onto whoever was destroying property at Big L' Ranch, and Raddix wanted it to end.

Raddix

Get to the station.

We've detained the group.

bustin' up the ranch

Hyperfocused on his screen, Raddix's thumbs quickly flew across his screen.

Be there soon.

"Sheriff McDugal has the culprits ruining the ranch. I have to head to the police station. Do you want to go?"

"Nah, I'm good. Thank you, though."

"Can I text you later?"

"Sure."

"Great. I think we need a do-over for this date." Raddix quickly kissed her on the cheek and disappeared down her stairs.

Chapter 21

"Raddix!" He stopped with his hand on his truck handle when Lily called. The pain in her eyes made him nervous.

"Miss me already?"

Lily smiled and hugged her middle, her eyes avoiding his. Raddix noticed the three troublesome grandmas staring at them across the way as Frank locked up the diner.

"We'll be the talk of the town by the time I get back to the ranch." Lily turned when Raddix jerked his head to the side. He smiled at her when she waved at them.

"Don't encourage those ladies. Trust me, they don't need it," Raddix said, laughing.

"I like them. They are eccentric, but their hearts are in the right spot."

Focusing his attention back on Lily, he asked, "Did you want to say something before I head out?"

"Um, yeah." She simultaneously clutched her throat and huffed out a breath. "I think we should consider this our third date and call it good."

He stared at her, unable to speak. His expression hardened. "What do you mean?"

"There's too much at stake for us to move forward."

Raddix shook his head, realizing the problem. "You're letting fear rule your life.'

"I'm making responsible decisions to keep *you* safe," Lily retorted, her words piercing his heart.

"Right," he let out a sarcastic chuckle. "Shouldn't I be the one to decide who and what I allow in *my* life?" When she didn't respond, Raddix continued, "You can call it whatever you want. Fear had you run from California. Fear had you change your name. Fear is keeping you awake at night. Fear is pulling you away from me."

"You don't even date women more than three times, so—"

"—Don't turn this on me." His voice rose, and with the lights from the diner, he could see they still had an audience, so he lowered his volume but not his emotion. "That's called deflecting, right?" He lifted his eyebrows in question.

He knew he conquered the answer when she crossed her arms across her chest, glaring at him, probably wishing her eyes were lasers that could disintegrate him where he stood.

"If you want to lie to yourself, Lily, I can't stop you, but I won't believe your lies. I know you like me and the ranch; probably the whole town knows I've fallen for you."

The urge to reach for her and pull her to his chest rendered him helpless. Instead, he popped his knuckles and stuffed his hands in his pockets, collapsing against his truck seat. "Take the time you need; figure out your feelings. I won't pressure you. When you're ready, come find me."

He swung his legs in the truck and slammed the door shut. Lily's eyes had filled with tears. If one drop fell, he wouldn't be able to leave the parking lot. "If you turn to God and give Him the fear you have, you'll be able to make better decisions for your life, overall."

"Thank you," she choked out.

"He wasn't sure if she was thanking him for the space or the advice, but either way, he was seconds away from hopping out of the truck and holding her the rest of the night.

That wouldn't win him any points right now. So, he put the truck in gear. "Lily, if you don't choose me," he cleared his throat, "it'll hurt like heck, but I'll get through it. I just want you to be happy."

He pressed hard on the accelerator and whipped out of the parking lot, gravel spinning under his wheels before his emotions let loose. *Lord, please be with Lily. Help her to trust in you. Keep her safe from any real threat, including herself. If it's your will, please let her choose me.*

Chapter 22

L ily grabbed her chirping cell phone, pressing the button on the side to silence it. Violet's name appeared in the banner at the bottom.

Are you ready?

Ugh! Lily had spent the last week fasting breakfast and praying, so going out to breakfast wasn't ideal. But she'd made these plans with Violet weeks ago before she'd turned her life back over to the Lord, and she liked the relationships she'd built with the folks in town. She knew God had placed her here for a reason.

Folks? She'd really become comfortable with her new life. She even talked like them now. Maybe it was all the praying she'd been doing. Lily spent most of her time in the Book of Psalms and Proverbs. She needed peace in her life even when she didn't understand the circumstances.

I'll meet you there in thirty minutes. Sorry, I actually slept a little bit.

Yay! Take your time.

Lily rolled over and opened her Bible to Proverbs 19, and read, "Fear of the Lord leads to life." The Bible had reminded her of unhealthy fear, which she'd been best friends with for months. That type of fear doubted God's power and goodness. She was ready to let God have all the power back.

Fifteen minutes later, she'd cleaned up and thrown on a pair of jean shorts and a seafoam green short-sleeved, v-neck shirt—Raddix's favorite color.

She texted Raddix, hoping things wouldn't be too awkward after a week of not speaking. He said he'd be patient, but people change their minds. She quickly pushed out the text and sent it before she could talk herself out of it.

Hey, how are you? Thanks for leading me back in the right direction. Maybe we could chat soon?

Lily stuffed her phone in her pocket, grabbed her wristlet and bounded out the door, her heart feeling content that all would be fine.

Cora saved Lily a seat between herself and her daughter, Willow. Today, Lily's heart felt light and free. She knew that God was in control of her life, and maybe she had left California out of fear, but she was meant to be in Haven Ridge. "You look different," Cora whispered in Lily's ear.

"Reconnecting with the Lord can do that," Lily replied with a smile.

Cora draped her arm around Lily's shoulders. "That makes me so happy. I've been praying for you. I don't know the specifics, but after we met, God told me to pray for you and I have every day."

"Thank you," Lily said as she pulled back, focusing on the new people at the table.

"So, Willow, you own the hair salon a few doors down?" Lily took a sip of her water.

"Yeah, my friend Val and I co-own the salon, and her sister, Harper, works for us. Growing up here, my mom cut my hair more often than not because she was too busy to drive me almost an hour for a haircut, so I figured the best way to give back to the town was to make the people living it look good."

Cora spoke up, "A mom's gotta do what she's gotta do."

Lily liked Willow already, which made sense. She was personable and fun, like her mom. Based on her clear, smooth skin, Lily assumed Willow was in her early twenties, but if genetics were any indication, she could be older and hide it well, like her mom. "I'll be in soon for sure."

Violet yelled to Lily from her spot, nearly halfway down and on the other side of the table. "Earl and Loretta have to go but wanted to say hi before they did.

The couple moved toward the door, where they greeted Lily with a hug and welcomed her to the group. In the corner, Lily thought she saw the same man from the flower shop who was buying roses for his girlfriend. An icy chill ran up her back.

Lord, give me strength. The Devil is going to do everything he can to let that fear back in. You are stronger, please don't let him win this. In Jesus name, Amen.

"So Earl, you deliver all the mail for the town?"

"Yes, Ma'am, I do." she loved the proudness in his voice. "That means I have to get going, but I hope you stick around. You're a great addition to this town."

"That's right, Dear. You are the best thing that's happened to Raddix Lawrence. That is one man who deserves happiness."

Lily pressed on her cheeks, trying to hide whatever color they were as she sat back down.

Randall sat directly across the table from her. He owned the only gas station and little grocery store in town. They'd always exchanged pleasantries when she was at the store, but getting to know him as part of this group felt special.

He lost his wife a couple of years ago. Said that God was the only thing keeping him going, and his son.

"I know that everyone in town, including myself, is happy that you're here with us." They shared a brief smile.

Frank, Hazel's husband and the owner of this establishment, came out once most of the group had left to clear the table. He was a large man in his late sixties or early seventies if Lily had to guess based on the crow's feet developing by his eyes.

But, the way he bounded around the tables, clearing them quickly and lifting the bucket holding all the dirty dishes, spoke of an energetic man half the owner's age. *Good thing, Hazel needs someone to keep up with her.*

Cora pressed the top end of her pen into her shoulder, allowing her to write down Frank's name as a food donor for the End of the Summer Festival. "Thank you."

"Any time." Frank hustled back into the kitchen.

Lily had signed up to run the dunk tank. They figured most of the folks in town would say yes to impress the new girl. She'd already started making a list in her head. Sheriff McDugal was first. *I mean, who doesn't want a chance to dunk the sheriff?* She wouldn't mind seeing Raddix get dunked, and hopefully, he wouldn't say no to her.

The three older ladies that Raddix referred to as the Troublesome Trio switched their original seats for ones next to Lily. "So dear, I don't mean to pry," Hazel started.

"Yes, she does," Frank interrupted. "All three of these women are called the Troublesome Trio for a reason.

"No one calls us that," Myrtle interjected. Lily didn't have the heart to correct the woman.

"Hush. Just ignore him," Hazel waved at Frank dismissively, but Lily saw the little kiss she blew him, making him blush.

Aw! That's adorable. I hope I find love like that. One that lasts well into my seventies.

Hazel continued. "We're sorry to hear that the sheriff didn't catch the people bustin' up Amelia's ranch. Raddix must be beside himself, having to fix things.

"Not that I'd mind watching him fix things on a hot day," Myrtle said, fanning her face with her hands.

"Oh, goodness, Myrtle, you're about thirty years too late for that one," Doris reprimanded.

Myrtle nonchalantly rolled her eyes. "My Gerald was the best man ever, but God hasn't taken my sight yet, and we have some mighty fine-looking cowboys in town for me to look at."

"Yup, that's why they are here, for *you* to look at," Doris stated sarcastically.

These women were a riot. Lily couldn't believe how much she liked them. She had Violet to thank for helping her become part of this community. Lily couldn't imagine ever leaving, regardless of what happened between her and Raddix.

Speaking of him, she pulled out her phone to see if she missed a text from him. She hadn't, but there was one from Amelia.

> **Hey, could you come by the ranch today for Emmanuel's session? The doctor just called with an appointment for tomorrow during your scheduled time.**

"Is that the hunk now?" Myrtle asked, wagging her eyebrows at Lily, causing her to break into a belly laugh.

"No, but it is Amelia, and she needs me to head to the ranch." Lily put her phone back in her pocket. "I had a blast today. You may be called the Troublesome Trio, but I think you are very entertaining."

"We aim to please, Dear," Hazel responded, smiling proudly.

Lily stood. "Before I leave. Do you have any advice for me on how to get people signed up for the dunk tank?"

"You better flirt like crazy," Myrtle laughed. "Only with Raddix, though. We wouldn't want that man to get in any fights and ruin his handsome face."

Lily shook her head at Myrtle's antics.

"Truthfully, start with the sheriff. He says yes every year, and maybe he can force his deputy's hand. Then, hit up everyone at the ranch," Hazel suggested.

Lily waved bye to the ladies and Frank, who was heading back out to the floor with an empty bucket to clean off more tables. The man in the corner booth still had the newspaper covering his face like she'd noticed when she'd said bye to Earl and his wife.

Lily ran across the street to her car, started it up, and pulled out toward the ranch. In her rearview, she saw the man leave the diner and get into a blue truck.

It seemed too convenient that he left at the same time she had, making her skin crawl. She was curious about the man, but all too quickly, she remembered the old saying: *Curiosity kills the cat.*

That didn't sit well with her, so she increased her speed, hoping she'd get to the ranch quickly and avoid the kill-the-cat part.

Chapter 23

The bright, blinding sun from earlier in the morning had taken a snooze behind the dark clouds. Raddix had dropped his phone in the creek when he let Blaze get a drink. Fortunately, Amelia offered to pick up the replacement he had ordered when she took Emmanuel to the doctor.

Raddix and his dad had just finished rotating the cattle through their many paddocks in time to start the afternoon livestock chores.

It's your day to muck the stalls, Dad. I'm going to stop here and feed the pigs and lambs, and then I'll meet you in the barn and start the milking."

"Sounds good, Son."

"Whoa, boy," Raddix pulled back on Blaze's reins and dismounted. He secured the horse's straps around the post before entering the pig's pen.

"Hey, piggies." Raddix called out, "Come and get your food."

Raddix spied the mama sow in her nest with her twelve piglets, now about three months old. Raddix recalled the busy spring Rocco, their veterinarian, had with all the births on the ranch. He was happy for Rocco and Renee when they took their kids on vacation, but he couldn't wait for him to return because he helped with the feedings to make sure the babies were growing appropriately.

After filling their food and water troughs, Raddix headed to the lambs. Most had been transitioned to the fields to graze with the sheep, but a few lambs remained in the barn. When Rocco returned, he'd check on all the babies born this past spring.

He was pleased to see that Alex and Allie finally filled the silage barrels in the barns. They even had more corn to prepare, so Amelia sent one of the ranch hands to Haven Ridge Outfitters for more storage drums.

"Raddix, where are you?"Amelia hollered as she and Quinton entered the lambs' headquarters.

He rounded the corner and immediately saw the concern etched on both their faces. "What's wrong?"

Quinton stepped forward. "Don't panic. We're not sure anything is wrong, but Lily's at the house and is pretty upset about a man she saw at the diner today. She said she's seen him before or something."

"Is she okay now?" *What was she doing at the diner? I thought she didn't eat out.*

"Yeah, I had her lay down in the guest room, and she passed out while we were talking. When she wakes up Emmanuel's already called dibs on her for their session, if she's up for it." Amelia shared.

"Quinton, I've got to cash in for the first time on that little side bet we had from the auction." Raddix would have gloated and enjoyed this much more if the circumstances were different. "I just finished here. Blaze needs to be brought back and brushed. The last thing left on my list today is taking care of the cows unless Dad has something; he's mucking out the stalls now. Can you find someone to finish up for me?"

"I'll take care of it for you, but please do something for me?" Quinton asked.

"What?"

"Go clean up. You stink, and Lily will not be impressed." Amelia playfully slapped her husband's bicep.

"Don't listen to him. If Lily's the one, she won't even flinch. It's okay to smell bad once in a while. It makes you all the more appealing when you're clean."

Both men pinned her with an are-you-serious look.

"Trust me, I know what I'm talking about," she said, pushing up to her toes and kissing her husband on the cheek.

Quinton engulfed Amelia in his arms, probably forgetting or just not caring that Raddix was still there.

He didn't need to see their make-out session. "Don't mind me; I'm leaving. Please don't forget about the cows and Blaze." Quinton and Amelia waved a hand in acknowledgment.

Raddix knew Amelia gave sound advice. Since Lily was sleeping anyway, he'd get cleaned up and hopefully have his own make-out session. That thought had Raddix jogging to his cabin.

Watching her sleep had convinced him even more that they needed a chance. Her flawless, soft skin looked peaceful, a feeling he knew was hard for her to achieve while awake. Her long blonde hair flowed along the pillow. Her petite body looked even smaller in the fetal position. Raddix forced himself to sit in the rocking chair instead of wrapping her in his arms, which was all he'd wanted to do since he entered the room.

Lily's stirring caused Raddix to charge toward her. He hoped she didn't kick him out or tell him she still wasn't ready to date. Instead, he wanted her to trust him and tell him her story. All he wanted to do was help her. Well, the make-out session he still desired, despite his cold shower, wasn't a bad idea either.

She bolted upright, pulling the cover up to her chin.

"Hey, it's me. You're okay." Raddix rushed to the bed. "Is it okay if I sit?" Raddix pointed to the side of the bed. When she slid over to make room, he slowly eased himself down.

"How'd you get out of work early?" Lily's soft voice pulled him in.

He tilted his head and let out a little chuckle. "Thanks to your generous auction bid, I can take whatever time I want off between now and the end of the year."

"I'm not following." Lily dropped the covers and hugged her knees.

"The men had a bet. Whoever had the highest auction bid could take any time off they wanted, and the others would have to find a way to cover it."

"Sounds like a bad deal for the losers. The winner could take advantage."

"It worked out well for me." Raddix rubbed a tendril of her hair between his fingers, leaning closer he could smell her fruity shampoo. Everything about this woman taunted him like a chokehold around his heart.

Gathering his self-control, he dropped her hair. "The bet was between Damon, my Dad, and I, so I wasn't worried. We're all hardworking, proud men. The ranchhands even agreed to fill in if necessary. They always want more work, but this is the first time I've asked, and Quinton helped me out." He shrugged his shoulders as if to say, *we're family*.

"You didn't answer my text." Lily blurted out.

"When did you text?" Happiness streaked through Raddix like a comet.

"This morning, after I realized you were right. I let fear run my life, but now I want to make Haven Ridge home."

The joy and energy filling Raddix's heart took over, and he clasped the back of her neck, pulling her lips to meet his in haste." It was a quick, hard kiss and not nearly long enough, but Raddix wanted to know more.

"More of that in a moment." Raddix wished he could speed up time when the blush rushed to her cheeks. "What happened today?"

"Besides getting to know everyone in town even better, including the Troublesome Trio, nothing. I did decide that I'm not going anywhere."

Raddix grinned and shook his head. He could only imagine what the ladies told Lily about him. He was definitely too afraid to ask. Why wasn't she telling him about the man?

"What else?" Raddix pushed.

"This man, who I think was the same one who creeped me out at the flower shop the last time your dad was there, hid behind a newspaper in a booth at the diner. As soon as I left, he did, too."

Raddix brushed it off. "That's probably James. He and his dad own and operate Haven Ridge Outfitters. He's shy and keeps to himself unless you speak to him."

A knock at the bedroom door interrupted them again. "Come in."

Emmanuel peered his head in the door. "Sorry, Raddix. It's my turn with Miss Lily unless she's not up to it. Which means you don't get her either because that wouldn't be fair."

The little boy's arms crossed over his chest, tilted head, and pursed-together lips were the cutest thing ever. As much as he wanted more time with Lily, he wouldn't take anything from Emmanuel.

"Uncle Raddix took the rest of the day off," Lily started.

"It's okay, Buddy." Raddix turned his attention to Lily. "Can we continue this later?" He kissed the top of her head as she answered.

"Sure."

"Mom, they're kissing again." Emmanuel hollered.

Raddix choked out a laugh. "Your day will come one day. You just wait, Little Man," Raddix promised as he left the room.

Raddix was definitely getting his alone time with Lily before sunset.

Chapter 24

"How's your week gone, Emmanuel?" Lily asked as they played a video game with all his favorite superheroes.

"Not so great, Lily," Emmanuel responded, using her same inquisitive tone.

"What happened?"

"Aw, I died. It's up to you now, Lily." Emmanuel had gained much of his energy back now that he was on a heavy medication dose to put him in remission. Lily remembered those early days and not wanting to talk about her disease; that made it all too real.

As Lily played, she repeated her question, but Emmanuel continued to focus on the video game, so Lily died on purpose. "Let's take a break from video games. Walk with me outside. The sun is good for you."

Emmanuel grumbled to himself but put away his controllers. "All right. Let's go." He stuffed his hands in his pockets.

"How come you didn't answer me when I asked what happened over the week?" She asked as they swung on the swings.

"Because I don't think it's fair, you ask all the questions, and I just have to answer them."

'Do you want to ask me questions too?"

A mischievous smile spread across Emmanuel's face as he nodded his head. "I go first. Who's your favorite superhero?"

"Iron Man," Lily responded, and Emmanuel jumped off his swing.

"What about Ghost Rider?" he asked aghast.

Lily slowed down. "If he's your favorite, that's okay, but mine is Iron Man."

"Yeah, I guess he's okay," Emmanuel always made her smile with his comments.

"My turn," Lily said as they walked the worn path toward the orchard. It also led to Raddix's cabin. She recalled the night of the cookout when she'd walked out to greet him. They'd come so far since then.

"What made your week not great?"

"I couldn't have any of the foods I wanted. It wasn't fair."

"Hmmm. I'm confused."

"About what?" Emmanuel asked.

Lily watched Emmanuel to see if his expression would change. "Based on what you said, it would be fair if you could eat whatever food you wanted, correct?"

"Mmm-hmm."

"Yet, your favorite superhero is Ghost Rider, who hands out punishments based on what the criminal deserves." When Emmanuel didn't make the connection on his own, Lily continued. "You see, Emmanuel, you deserve to live pain-free, and the only way to do that is by eating certain foods and avoiding getting sick. It wouldn't be fair if you ate the food you *wanted*, and it hurt you."

Lily always tried to make connections to the kiddo's interests so they would be more vested in the sessions. It sounded like a great analogy in her head, but maybe it was a bit of a stretch for Emmanuel.

"Before the doctor said I could eat treats when I'm in remission. We see him again tomorrow, maybe he'll say I can have treats?"

"How are you feeling about that?" Lily asked as they reached the row of greenhouses. Emmanuel turned back without warning.

Lily's heart wept when Emmanuel's eyes drooped. "I'm scared I'm not better. Can I die from this?" Emmanuel picked a dandelion and handed it to Lily.

"Aw, thanks, Emmanuel." Lily smiled on the outside, but her heart bled for this little boy. "My doctors have always told me that Crohn's Disease itself doesn't kill people. Complications from the disease are what shorten people's lives."

"Like what," Lily knew Emmanuel would continue asking questions until he was satisfied.

"If you have strictures—"

"—I don't have any of those," Emmanuel blurted out.

"That's good. You don't want any scars. They can be one of the biggest problems for people with Crohn's." Lily didn't want to share with him about the possibility of atrophy to the heart muscle or surgeries to correct abdominal issues. Still, she'd be sure to let Amelia and Quinton know it might be essential to let him get all his questions answered at the doctor's tomorrow.

"Miss Lily," Emmanuel squinted one eye as he looked up at her, but the sun must have been too much. Looking back at the ground, he asked, "Do you have any strictures?"

Lily heard the caring in his voice. He was the most empathic little boy she'd ever met. In fact, he had more empathy for others than some adults she knew who didn't have an ASD diagnosis. "Not that I am aware of, but they can develop. Last week, I had to get medicine because my stomach was in pain. Stress is not our belly's friend. I get tested every two years to make sure nothing new has developed. You'll be tested yearly or every other year, too."

"Great, I'll have to have the camera again?"

"Afraid so, but your doctor will tell you exactly when, so try not to think about that, or you may hurt your belly."

"Twenty-three nineteen." Emmanuel grabbed his stomach and bent at the waist.

"What does that mean?" Lily's chest heaved rapidly.

"Sharp pain, sharp pain." Emmanuel cried.

They were too far away from the main house for him to walk. She couldn't leave him alone while she ran for help. *Lord, give me the strength to carry this boy who is almost as tall as me."*

"Let's go." Lily scooped him up and started walking as quickly as possible. With one arm still enclosed around his middle, Emmanuel gripped her neck with the other.

Lily focused on praying since worrying about the burn in her biceps and legs wouldn't help. *Where are all the cowboys when you need one? It's past lunchtime, not quite time for dinner. Raddix took the rest of the day off . . . Lord, forgive me. Thank you for allowing me to help Emmanuel, but if a cowboy came to help right now, I wouldn't complain.*

The main house finally came into her view. She'd passed at least three barns, and the butcher shop was the next building. She could stop there. Jeff could help. But what if he wasn't there? She just needed to keep walking.

"You okay?" Lily asked as she wiped the sweat from her forehead on her shoulder.

"The pain is still sharp."

Dear God, please help him. Give me the pain if someone has to have it.

Once she passed the barn with horses, she saw the silhouette of two cowboys leaving the corral. They both came running. *Thank you, God!*

Raddix and Quinton reached Lily at the same time. Quinton pulled Emmanuel from Lily's arms. "He has a sharp pain."

"Is it still bad?" Quinton asked him.

"It's getting better, thanks to Miss Lily."

Lily let out a huff. "Oh no, it was all God."

"I'm going to get him in the house. Thank you, Lily." Quinton carried him like a balloon filled with helium.

Here she was, taking slow, controlled breaths so she wouldn't pass out.

Raddix swooped Lily off the ground, and a little squeal escaped her. "What are you doing?"

"Carrying you to the house," Raddix replied.

"Why?" Lily didn't even wait for his answer. "Put me down," Lily commanded with a smile.

"Do I have to?"

"Please." Raddix's arms framed around her hadn't done anything to regulate her heartbeat.

He set her feet on the ground and lifted her chin with his finger. Their mutual gaze caused Lily's stomach to dip and her heart to skip a beat. He reached for her hand, one finger at a time, and laced them together. Placing his other hand behind her neck, he pulled her closer.

"Can we get back to where we were earlier?" He whispered.

"Uh, huh," she managed. His crooked grin made him even more attractive.

Gripping his biceps, Lily pushed to her toes and pressed her lips to Raddix's. She couldn't believe she kissed him, but he responded with a fiery passion. She melted into him, wishing this moment would never end.

He pulled back, nuzzling his nose into her neck, pushing her hair away, and planting kisses along her neck and down to her collarbone. Her breath quickened as goosebumps rose on her skin.

She wasn't sure how long it'd been since he stopped kissing her. When she slowly opened her eyes, he was studying her.

"You are gorgeous," he whispered, cupping her face and kissing her again. This time, it was more methodical. With each sweet kiss, she felt his love and care. For the first time in a long time, she finally felt safe.

Chapter 25

"Do you think this will work, Quinton?" Raddix asked as he pulled the barbed wire tight around the newest broken post.

"It's got to be better. Sheriff McDougal isn't giving us any hope that these people will be caught," Quinton said as he threw on a pair of gloves and helped Raddix pull the wire even tighter.

"He let the kids from a few weeks ago leave without consequence. They admitted that someone offered them money to vandalize our property. Why didn't he use the kids as bait so we could catch whoever ordered this?"

"Good question."

Quinton positioned a trail camera on the closest post and checked his phone to make sure it was set up and working while Raddix picked up their materials.

"I still feel like whatever Lily isn't telling me is connected to the attacks on the ranch."

"Anything's possible, Raddix. Maybe you should try talking to her again. She might be in a better place to talk about it," Quinton suggested.

Raddix scoffed. "Doubtful. This guy in town who creeped her out at the flower shop and the diner seems to disappear for days on end. I thought it might have been James, but I took Lily into Outfitters the other day, and she said it wasn't him."

He pressed on his knuckles, one at a time. "McDugal said there isn't anything he can do because the guy hasn't done or said anything to Lily except for that first time at the flower shop when he asked for roses for his girlfriend."

"Interesting. No one has seen him with a girl?"

"No. Lily doesn't like roses, so it all seems. . . fishy." Raddix huffed out a frustrated breath.

"What did the doctor have to say about Emmanuel's sharp pains? He seems to be better now."

Quinton slammed the tailgate shut as the men hopped into the truck. "He increased Emmanuel's steroid to get him into remission. That should make the sharp pains subside. He'll start infusions in six or seven weeks and can come off the steroid. Honestly, it's way too much for my brain to handle." He slammed the steering wheel.

Raddix saw the pain, frustration, and love in the man's eyes. Emmanuel was his pride and joy.

"Sorry. It's hard. I have to be strong for Amelia and Emmanuel, but sometimes, when I'm away, I have to let it out," Quinton's voice trembled.

Raddix slapped Quinton on the shoulder. "I can only imagine, Man. Whatever you need, I'm here for you."

Amelia had invited Lily for dinner. She brought chocolate chip cookies, Raddix's favorite, though she brought them because they were Emmanuel's favorite, too, and he had asked her for them.

It was amazing how strong steroids were. After a couple of days of at the higher dose, Emmanuel was the life of the party, talking nonstop, of course, about superheroes and video games. When he got interested in something, he studied it until he knew everything about it, and then, much to everyone else's chagrin, he talked about it constantly.

As impressive as Emmanuel's knowledge was, the other kids' ability to act interested in the subject matter or, at the very least, not say anything mean was equally impressive. Raddix knew that repeatedly talking about the same thing or reenacting the same scene from a movie got frustrating. He didn't know how Amelia and Quinton did it.

Raddix leaned over and whispered in Lily's hair, "Want to take a walk after dinner?"

"Definitely," she breathed.

Amelia called everyone's attention. "I know this might come as a shock to some of you, but Alex and Allie have decided to move in with her mom, so they'll be leaving us in a couple of weeks. Quinton and I will care for the orchards, gardens, and greenhouses until we hire someone.

Raddix felt bad for Jeff and Katy. The point of raising your kids on a ranch like this was to stay together, but now their only child was leaving to live with his in-laws. He wasn't a dad, but he could only imagine not liking it if it were his kid leaving.

"Would you rather clean up the table on your own or stick your head in the toilet?"

"Emmanuel!" Quinton called from across the kitchen. "All of you are cleaning the table, and there won't be anyone's head in the toilet tonight." His newest obsession was playing Would You Rather.

Everyone worked together to clean up, including the adults. Raddix took advantage of the tight quarters near the sink. He placed one hand on Lily's hip and the other on the countertop in front of her. "Sorry, Ma'am, there's too much traffic in here, so I'll park myself right near you." Her giggle reverberated through his chest.

"Would you rather do the Spiderman kiss with me or kiss your dad?" Emmanuel asked Darlene.

"Quinton, what are you teaching this boy?" Damon asked with a hint of humor in his voice.

"Not me. Blame her." Quinton laughed, pointing at Lily, pulling her attention away from Raddix.

"What did I do?" Raddix was going to ask, but she beat him to it. He loved how she fit right in with his family.

"If you give Emmanuel something to work towards, he'll be more apt to achieve his goals," Quinton mocked Lily.

"I don't sound like that," she retorted, then whispered to Raddix, "Do I?"

He shook his head.

"He's achieving his goals alright and watching YouTube when he does. Don't even get me started on the Spiderman 3 Toby McGuire dance."

Emmanuel pulled on the front of his shirt and clapped his hands together, and Quinton stepped in just before his son could finish the dance with his hips. "That's enough."

Raddix turned away, biting the inside of his cheek. Quinton would give him extra work if he laughed right now. It didn't help that Lily was scraping her lower lip with her teeth, presumably to stop herself from laughing, but that act had every single nerve ending in Raddix's body on high alert.

Saved by the text. Raddix pulled his phone from his pocket. Sheriff Mc-Dugal's name appeared across his screen.

Raddix

I think we have them.

Come to the station.

"Hey, McDugal has the the vandalizers, supposedly. Do you want me to follow you home as I head to the station?"

"Nah, I want to stay here a little longer if that's okay."

Raddix kissed her forehead. "It's more than okay. I'll text you when I'm done." He kissed her cheek. "We're not getting that make-out session today."

"What make-out session?" Lily asked, shocked.

"The one I've been dreaming about all day."

Lily fiddled with the front of his shirt, only to tug him closer. He could feel her warm breath on his face. "I like to make dreams come true, so maybe you should stop by when you're done instead of calling."

Shocked, he took a moment to register what Lily had just said. Just before he could respond, she kissed him, slow and sweet.

She only pulled away when Emmanuel hollered, "They're doing it again."

Raddix whispered in her ear, "You are a tease."

"It's only teasing when you don't follow through."

"I'll hurry," Raddix said his goodbyes and flew out the door. Looking back, he could only see Lily's bright smile. He wouldn't mind seeing that for the rest of his life.

Chapter 26

The cool evening air was invigorating after the heat from the day. Despite Lily's ride from the ranch, her head still spun. She couldn't wait until Raddix arrived. She'd tell him all about her past, let her know she wouldn't let fear keep them apart, and then the making out could begin.

The moon shone on Lily's door as she ascended the stairs. She must be seeing things. Lily slowed her pace, studying the door from afar. Justice would be served tonight. The men defacing the ranch's property would finally be apprehended and charged, whatever the process was, to make sure they didn't cause any more trouble for her new friends.

Hopefully, Raddix was still interested in being more than friends. What if he didn't want anything to do with her once he found out? The idea of him dying because he hung out with her made Lily's stomach churn, but so did the possibility of him not wanting to try. She'd have to worry about all that later. With eyes fixated on the slightly ajar door, Lily took another step.

Last week, before Raddix showed up for their date, Lily received a call from the detectives back home, telling her that they'd lost all connection with the *alleged* stalker. "It's like he disappeared into thin air," were his only comments.

The nerve of that detective. The stalker, the one *they'd* lost track of, had threatened to kill her and any man she dated. How dare he make it seem like this was all in her mind. The debilitating fear this entire situation had caused was *not* in her head. She was a therapist for crying out loud. She wouldn't have left a relatively nice guy and year-round sunshine for a place she'd freeze in just a few short months.

Lily looked around, searching the dark night, listening for footsteps of an assailant fleeing the scene or heavy breathing from someone hiding out, but nothing of the sort came. Instead, the peaceful sound of crickets filled the night air.

What if someone was in the therapist's apartment? Wouldn't Violet have heard something? Lily's apartment was right above her landlord's. Surely, she would have called Lily to warn her, or she would have called the police. Heck, she might have even called Sean, Raddix's dad, since they seemed chummy lately—her words, not Lily's.

Lily pressed her back to the house and slowly moved up the steps, hoping she missed every squeak and creak she'd grown accustomed to since she moved here.

Lily's heart thumped against her ribs, and all she could hear was her blood rushing through her body. Sweat formed at Lily's brow. She wasn't prepared for this. How had he found her?

No! Don't start that again. She scolded herself.

The logical answer was that she didn't latch the door well enough, and the wind blew it open. There weren't any dig marks on the door. The jamb wasn't busted. Her mind was playing tricks on her again.

Despite the hollowed-out feeling in her stomach, she told herself to stop being ridiculous and pushed open her front door. She flicked on the light and scanned the room while her feet remained frozen just beyond the threshold.

Her apartment was silent as a graveyard, calming her nerves, none. Lily took one step forward, allowing herself space to close the door. She toe-heeled off her sneakers to show herself that everything was fine and she'd stay put in her apartment, not running away.

"Lord, please show yourself." The usually welcomed silence now had an eerie feeling in the pit of her stomach, her mouth dry as the Sahara. Something didn't feel right.

Lily grabbed a glass of water and down it. Setting the empty glass upside down to dry, Lily heard a thump, sending a bolt of fear straight to her heart. She turned around in a panic, clutching the counter behind her, she sucked in a breath.

Her chest heaved with rapid, short breaths, but nothing else moved. Her feet were frozen. She should have run out the front door, down to Violet's, and called the police, but she couldn't move. That, coupled with the fact that she didn't want to bring harm to her sweet landlady.

She strained her ears to hear past her ragged breathing. Another thump.

Without hesitating, she grabbed the giant knife from the butcher block. She clutched her fingers around it, ready to attack. She might have laughed at how silly she looked if she wasn't so scared. The famous shower scene from Alfred Hitchcock's Psycho movie came to mind. Too bad she hated horror movies and had never seen that one. How had it ended? How would this end for her?

Thankfully, this was a small apartment. The kitchen/living room combo was clear. She couldn't imagine the thumping was coming from the bathroom so that only left her bedroom.

Side-stepping with her back an inch away from the wall, she groped the wall with her free hand as she worked her way to her bedroom.

Lily's body tremored worse than the three-point-eight earthquake she'd experienced last year, nearly demolishing everything she owned, which wasn't much, making it easier for her to move to Montana.

The light thump startled her again. She halted in her spot. Her eyes flew to the left and the right. Nothing. The closer she got to her bedroom, she could hear the sound coming from her closet—the slightest tap against the left wall, then the right.

Anger replaced her fear. She would show this monster he couldn't control her anymore. She burst into her room, flicked on the light, and threw open her closet door. Instantly, she dropped the knife. Her hands shook violently as she screamed.

She stepped back slowly, wishing to unsee what hung from a rope in her closet. Tearing her gaze from the swinging rope, rose, and the note, she stumbled backward, ramming into the wall behind her. Tears replaced her screams.

The sound of police sirens had her already racing heart fulminating out of control. *This isn't good.*

Her first instinct was to run, get away, and protect the friends she'd met here. "Goodbye, Raddix," Lily whispered, not bothering to hide the anguish in her voice.

Chapter 27

"Raddix, calm down," Sheriff McDugal ordered. "If you don't get yourself under control, I'll have to send you home."

Deputy Williams placed his hands in front of Raddix's chest but didn't make contact, which Raddix appreciated.

This investigation had taken a turn Raddix hadn't expected. Based on Sheriff McDugal's hinged jaw, neither had he.

For fifteen minutes, Raddix paced the entryway of the small police station, waiting for more information.

A strange feeling that he'd never felt before washed over him. He wanted Lily by his side. She was finally dropping the walls around her heart. Then he was dragged away, for what? Nothing.

He could be holding Lily in his arms right now. That's not to say he didn't want to catch these guys, but that didn't look like what would happen tonight.

"Is there any more news?" Raddix asked when Deputy Williams slid behind the front desk.

"Sheriff McDugal wants you to meet him in his office."

He paced in that room for another five minutes before the sheriff arrived.

"What's the verdict," Raddix turned on his heels when the door opened.

"More teenagers who say they don't have a clue who paid them to bust your posts down. He said there was a man and a woman this time. They both mentioned Amelia by name, but I'm unsure how that fits yet."

"Do they live around here? What *do* you know?"

The sheriff raised his eyebrows in warning, but Raddix didn't really care. This needed to stop now.

"They live over an hour away. One of the boys is sixteen. He's the oldest." They both shared a look, knowing that none of them would be held accountable as an adult for their actions. They kept the damage just enough to be miserable but not a federal crime. Interesting. That felt intentional.

"So we're no closer than we were before?" Raddix hadn't meant it as a question, but that's how it came out.

"Act-u-a-lly," the sheriff enunciated, "the boys said that they have done other things."

"At the ranch?"

"Yes. I told you secret evidence helps us." The sheriff smiled, all proud. Raddix didn't want to point out that he shouldn't be too proud because he still didn't have a clue who was destroying their property. Yeah, fixing the damage was a pain. Even worse was when Amelia said that she was happy it was them. Happy? Seriously? She knew other ranches in the area that wouldn't be able to afford to fix the continual damage. Which was true, but who was she kidding? Amelia would have sent one of us to whatever ranch needed the help and told us to fix it for them.

"A different person. A woman, one they'd never seen before and hadn't seen since she stumbled upon them while they were busting the post before. She gave them the rose to put by the barn."

"What? The events are linked?" realization hitting Raddix like a hurricane-force wind across the face—this must not be connected to Lily's stalker if a woman wanted the rose there. "They couldn't ID the the woman?"

"It was dark. She had a full *bank robber's mask* on as the boys described it, but he said he thought he saw a hint of blonde in the cutout for the eyes."

The man Lily described has sandy blonde hair. Perhaps they mistook the person for a woman?

"There are at least two people who want to make the ranch or, according to the boys, Amelia, suffer. They don't seem interested in harming you guys, but things can change quickly, especially when we don't know who we're dealing with."

"Go home. Still, keep the information about the rose and the mention of Amelia's name to yourself. I think that will still be the key to finding the identity of at least one of the culprits."

Raddix glanced at his watch as he walked to his truck. Was it too late to drop in on Lily? He definitely wanted to, but if she was sleeping, he didn't want to disturb her, knowing how hard it was for her at night. He'd texted her and waited in his truck to see what she thought.

He'd sent five texts over the last ten minutes. No response. All he knew was that his messages had been delivered, as indicated underneath his previous text.

His truck roared to life. He wasn't waiting anymore.

Arriving at Lily's house in record time, Raddix took the stairs two at a time. He rapped on her door, noting that the kitchen light illuminated the space inside. He couldn't see any sign of Lily through the thin curtain over the door window. When another round of knocks went unanswered, he tried the door. Unlocked. Why? Lily wouldn't do that, would she?

Before he could call out, he heard her crying. When he turned the corner, he saw her lying on the floor in the fetal position. Kneeling, he pulled her shoulders close to him. "You'll be okay. I'm here."

"Raddix? No, you have to go. Get out of here now!" she screamed against his chest and then fell limp in his arms.

Chapter 28

"Lily! Lily!" Raddix shook her gently. "Do you hear me?"

"Yes, I do," she mumbled. "I feel you, too. Why are you shaking me?"

She pushed off Raddix's chest. "Why are you here?"

"You told me to come by when I finished. I texted, but you didn't respond." Raddix dropped his hands.

"Texts?" Lily said, confused. "I didn't get any texts from you."

"Where's your phone?"

"I don't know," she admitted. Then she remembered the mannequin wearing wearing a cowboy hat, the rose, and the note:

YOU DIDN'T LISTEN. NOW RADDIX WILL SUFFER. YOU ARE MINE AND ALL MINE. WE'LL BE TOGETHER SOON.

"You need to leave. You are in danger." She frantically pushed him away.

Raddix circled his arms around her, making her warm like a cocoon, "I'm never leaving you."

"I left the ranch late. The adults were playing cards, and I lost track of time. When I came back, my door was opened. It didn't seem like foul play, so I came in." Lily took a deep breath.

She continued with the replay for Raddix until she reached the end. She'd developed bumps on her flesh, and the gentle way he rubbed them off hadn't gone unnoticed.

When she finished, Raddix cleared his throat. "Where's the knife you were holding?"

Her eyes searched her surrounding area but came up with nothing. "I don't know."

"Did you close your bedroom closet again?" he asked skeptically.

Noting it was closed, she hissed, "I must have." She popped to her feet. Raddix quickly followed.

"I'm not crazy," she yelled at him. How many times had she heard her patients say the same thing?

He held up his hands in surrender. "I never said you were. I'm just trying to get the full picture of what happened before you call Sheriff McDugal."

"I'm not calling him." Panic spread throughout her entire body. Her high-pitched voice continued, "He said if I ever did contact the police, he'd take care of me right away."

Raddix let out a sound Lily didn't appreciate. She knew what was coming. "Is it possible you collapsed into a deep sleep? You said that you barely sleep. A body can't sustain that."

Was that possible? Lily knew it was plausible. Exhausted people had just fallen where they stood. Is that what had happened to her?

"Will you check my closet, please?"

Raddix released his grip on her shoulders. Her gaze locked on him. *Was he nervous?* His hand clutched the knob and blew out a hard breath.

"Raddix?"

"I'm good." He inched the door open one measurement at a time. Once the door fully exposed the inside, Raddix's hand fell.

"What? Do you see it? The body? The note? The rose?"

Sheer panic filled his rugged features, the color drained from his face, and she saw it—empathy in his eyes. He didn't believe her. She shuffled her feet toward her closet. Peeking over the open door, she saw the boxes she hadn't unpacked and her few clothes hanging from plastic hangers.

Everything she'd seen before wasn't anywhere in sight. She sat back into her heels and pressed her forehead into the carpet.

Her shoulders shook. She couldn't hold her sobs in any longer.

Raddix enveloped her. "Talk to me, Lily."

She shook her head.

"I wish you would trust me." He guided her into his arms and cradled her with more affection than she'd thought he was capable of. Then he tenderly slid his fingers through her hair. Her spine shivered.

"I don't want anything to happen to you."

Raddix scoffed. "Nobody can hurt me. except for you. I need to know what's going on so I can protect you. If anything happens to you. I will never be the same.

He gently drew circles on the back of her hand with his thumb.

"I don't have much to offer. One day, I got roses delivered to my door with a note that read, "I want to know everything about you." It had a cute little smiley face and a heart. It was handwritten, so I figured whoever got them for me also dropped them off. I first thought they had to be from River, the man I was seeing then."

Raddix inhaled loudly. For some reason, this made Lily feel wanted and desired in a good way. He gestured for her to keep going. She smiled inwardly.

She swallowed down the bile that inches it was into her throat just by allowing her brain to relive the few dreaded days of her stalker's relentless behavior before she left.

With as much strength as she could pull off, she continued. "River had been gone for a few days for work. He couldn't receive calls. It was a retreat and team-building getaway with the company."

"Hmm"

Lily's back rumbled against his chest. "What?"

"Seems convenient. Don't mind me. Keep going," he urged, gently brushing his hands up and down the length of her arms.

"Every day, I received more roses with sweet notes." Lily paused. "When River returned, we went out for a nice dinner and walk on the beach," Raddix growled this time, making Lily chuckle softly. "The next day, I got one single rose, which was dead. The note revealed his desire to have me to himself and kill any man he saw me with and then kill me if I didn't listen."

She blew out a breath. Raddix squeezed her tight against his chest, giving her the strength to carry on. "He disclosed that he'd been in my house. I couldn't stay there any more. Besides, I didn't want anyone to get hurt because of me, so I left."

"Do you have any idea speculation of who it might be?"

"No. I was working mainly from home, only seeing a few clients out in the community. I only interacted with my boss, River, and a few ladies I'd grown up with. That's how I met River"

"And how long had you known River?"

"Not long six or seven months."

Lily turned and studied Raddix's face. His eyebrows were pulled close together and his lips curled inward.

"You can hate me if you want after this, but I'm calling the sheriff since you won't. But first, I'm calling Quinton and my dad. I need a day off tomorrow."

She blinked, feeling confused, as Raddix strolled away. Her stomach had been in knots for so long; she wasn't sure what normal felt like anymore. Maybe this would be a good thing. The sheriff could deal with the detectives, then she wouldn't have to. They all talked cop lingo that she didn't care to learn.

Lily only heard the last part of his conversation, with whom she assumed was Quinton, as she lumbered into the room.

"I'll do the last haying of the season, not that I need to, you know, with me winning the bet and all," he chuckled.

There was a long pause. She didn't want Raddix to have to work harder later on in order to stay here now.

"Thanks, Man. We'll be over at some point tomorrow. McDugal wants to talk with her then, too."

Raddix jerked his head toward the couch, and Lily obliged, missing the safety from earlier that she'd felt being in Raddix's arms.

She leaned back against his solid chest and relished in his arms, which embraced her waist. Perfect fit. Lily was meant to be in Raddix's world. He held his large, calloused hand palm up. The invitation made her heart swell. Her soft skin against his ignited every nerve in her body, reminding her of the Mission Impossible match striking a trail of fire. She exhaled, trying to calm her nerves.

"Are you okay?"

That was a loaded question. Tears pricked at the back of her eyes, ready to spill out any moment. She swallowed, trying to coat her dry throat. No luck. Fear pricked at her. Stress could negatively affect any person's health. Stress for a person with Crohn's was even more debilitating. Her stomach had been feeling the effects of her stress lately, but tonight, it felt like someone had knifed her repeatedly. She'd be lucky if the contents within her stomach stayed put, but she wasn't making any promises. That, coupled with her growing fear that somehow the stalker would harm Raddix, was the reason she'd wanted him to leave.

"I'm not sure yet." Selfishly, it felt like heaven being in his arms. She'd dread talking with the sheriff tomorrow, but for tonight, she would enjoy this moment with Raddix.

It very well could be their last moment together.

Chapter 29

“It felt so real.”

“I'm sure it did.” Raddix tenderly stroked her blonde hair, briefly connecting with her toned shoulder, lighting his insides up.

The hold this woman had taken over him scared him. Would he ever be able to freely love her without fear of losing her? He knew Lily was special when they met in July. All the last eight weeks had done was reinforce his desire for this woman.

Aggression had built up in his chest while Lily shared her secret. She had a stalker. How would he keep her safe? If he ever found this coward, he'd stomp on him harder than an agitated bull on the loose.

Not that Raddix *wanted* to hear the details of what he was about to ask, but he had to know before he revealed his growing feelings.

"Tell me about River." That came out more authoritative than he'd meant. "I mean if you want to or think it will help." Hopefully, that sounded less like a jealous meathead and more like a man who wanted to build a relationship with her.

"Are you sure?" You seemed to tense up quite a bit just saying his name." The long pause must have been enough of an answer for her. She tilted her head toward him; that was all the invitation he needed. He pressed his lips onto hers—warm and soft. He slid his fingertips down her exposed neck with his hand. Her shiver gave him the courage to press on. He deepened the kiss, releasing the passion and desire he'd held inside for too long.

Lily responded exactly how he wanted. She turned into him, glided her palms up his chest, and fisted the back of his hair. A little moan escaped from her at the same time a growl, deep from within Raddix exploded and he intensified the kiss.

She pressed her palm on his chest and gently pulled away. "I'm not complaining, but I do need to breathe. Wow."

"I'll take that as a compliment." Raddix hadn't dropped his hand from her face. He slowly traced the outline of her lips with his thumb. "I'm falling for you, Lily."

Her eyes widened slightly before she fixed her features. *What had I done?* Maybe she loved the guy and was just waiting until McDugal caught the stalker to return to him.

"What if I fell for you long ago, but I'm not willing to put you in harm's way, and you don't date women more than three times, so I don't see how this could work." Lily turned around, probably so she didn't have to face him.

When she tried to escape his arms, he pulled her back against his chest. "Please let me help you. I won't kiss you again." He paused, realizing that sounded so final and was the opposite of what he was going for. "Unless you want me to." She tenderly elbowed his side, making him laugh.

"Go ahead, tell me about River. I'll be a good listener this time."

She turned her head toward him again. "Ok. Last time, it seemed like you were marking your territory."

"When you look at me like that, Woman, it's hard not to kiss you."

A few seconds ticked by while he recovered his breathing. Raddix put his hands on either side of her head and faced her forward. "If you don't want me to kiss you, you can't look at me like that."

"Like what?"

"Just go on with the story." Raddix had to stop talking about kissing since that's all he was thinking about. Holding her against his skin with that combination was lethal.

"We'd only dated a couple of times. He was nice."

"Is "nice" a good thing or a bad thing?" Raddix asked, honestly trying to understand Lily's thoughts and feelings.

"We would probably still be dating if I hadn't left."

Raddix's heart dropped. Could this be considered *stealing another man's woman?* He'd <u>never</u> be *that man.* "Oh."

"Raddix," Lily said in a hushed tone. His breath hitched. Man, he loved the way his name sounded on her lips. "I'm glad I came here. She rested her hands on his hands, which were on her stomach.

"I wish you would have told me. There's so much I would have changed."

"Like what?" Lily's soft voice felt like a punch in the gut now that he wondered if he could really have her.

"I wouldn't have let you run alone or live here alone. I would have protected you. I could have done nothing differently about falling for you, but that's my problem, not yours."

Lily faced him again. He was a complete goner. *Lord, I know you and my mom . . . You both ganged up on me and put this beautiful woman in my life. Thanks for helping me realize how great she would be for me. Don't let her be taken from me so soon.*

"I don't ever plan on returning to California. I like the life I've started to build here."

He punched a fist in the air, hollering. The urge to kiss her took over, but he kept true to his word. Leaning closer until he was within an inch of her lips. "You want me to kiss you, don't you?"

Lily pulled away slightly with a smirk on her kissable lips. "Hmm. I'm not sure. I might have to think about that."

"Woman, you're killing me." He let his body flail back against the couch, arms spread wide.

"Thank you for making me feel safe." Lily's silken voice unraveled him, but not nearly as much as her pulling him up by the front of his shirt and pressing her lips to his.

Without hesitation, his greedy mouth took control, pressing his upper body flush with her. He guided the elastic the rest of the way out of her hair to weave his fingers through the blonde silk on the back of her neck.

When Lily wrapped her arms around his shoulders, it felt like she'd melted into him, forgetting about the stress and fear of having a stalker. He'd do anything to make Lily happy and protect her.

He felt a sudden joy that he knew only existed because the Lord had given him Lily. He'd never wanted a woman the way he desired for her.

Lily sunk her head into the pillowy couch, creating enough room to turn her head. "Must . . . have . . .air."

"Sorry." Raddix straightened and drew her body to him, nuzzling his face into her neck. He whispered into her hair, I'm not afraid of a stalker. The only thing I fear is losing you." Raddix kissed her knuckles. "I just have one request. Please don't break my heart."

Why had I said that last part? His mom's death destroyed his dad. The last thing he wanted was to understand what his dad had endured. Lily pulled away with eyes full of compassion.

"Raddix, I'd never do that on purpose."

"Your mom didn't hurt your dad on purpose."

"I know," he admitted, his heart not feeling the same confidence." Raddix met her eyes. "You won't up and leave me like you did River, will you? I promise I'll do everything I can to protect you."

Lily placed her palm over his scruffy cheek. "You are a good man, Raddix. Thank you." She laid her head on his chest, allowing him to wrap her in his arms.

Joy rippled through Raddix. He would savor this feeling for a long time.

Chapter 30

She sat up suddenly, causing Raddix to do the same and banging their heads together. "Ouch," Raddix rubbed his head. "Are you okay, Darlin'?" he asked, kissing her forehead.

Lily swung her legs to the floor and stretched her arms over her head. "How'd you sleep?"

"Great. You?"

"Liar." Lily accused as her back protested against her standing position.

Raddix stood and stretched right next to her. "Holding you in my arms while we sleep is great, so you'll never hear me complain about that. Besides, I usually get up when the sky is still black, so this was a treat." He pointed to the sun that shot through the undressed window.

"How about I make breakfast? We'll clean up and then head to the ranch," Lily suggested as she stepped toward the kitchen.

Lily squealed when Raddix wrapped his arms around her middle, preventing her from moving forward. He rested his chin on her shoulder. "I have a better idea. You go shower, and I'll make you breakfast. What can you have?"

His awareness of her disease felt intimate. "I have homemade waffles that I've frozen. Try reheating them in the air fryer so it gets crispy."

"Try?" He spun her around. Looking into his eyes this early in the morning was a surefire way to cut her productivity for the day in half. . . at minimum.

Sleeping in Raddix's arms was pure joy. Maybe it wasn't the most comfortable for her back, but Lily had slept through the night for the first time in months. She hadn't jerked awake every ten minutes or less like every other night when she'd dozed off. He was her melatonin.

"Yeah, I've never done it before, so we'll see how it comes out." Skepticism filled his features. "I try many things most people won't if it makes life easier for me. I've never gone hungry if that counts for anything."

He nodded. Relief traveled across his handsome features. "I'm willing to try anything with you." A slow grin, one that Lily would pay another few thousand dollars to see, pulled at one corner of Raddix's mouth. "Look at the bright side; if it doesn't work or tastes bad, we can eat whatever Carolyn and Cash have left at the Ranch."

"Great Idea." Lily stopped on the threshold between the kitchen and the short hallway leading to the bathroom and her room. She spun on her heels to find Raddix's feet frozen to where she left him. "Thank you for keeping me safe."

"Always."

With that one word, her heart sang with joy.

Lily felt like the poster child for quick life changes. It was still hard to believe that it had only been a couple of months since she'd picked up her entire life in less than twenty-four hours and moved from California to Montana. Driven by fear for her life and for River's, a stalker had ripped her positivity and carefree attitude away from her.

A few minutes after she'd let the water from the showerhead pound on her shoulders, Raddix had knocked. Yelling through the door, he'd said they needed to leave soon. Somebody hit the ranch again.

She finished and dressed quickly. Rushing out the door, she was happy the ranch never lacked a supply of delicious food that she could eat.

"I'm sorry we didn't get to see if your waffles taste good reheated. Maybe that can be our next dinner together or breakfast?" His subtle wink as they buckled up and his engine roared to life almost set off fireworks in her belly.

"I might have to make you fresh waffles if you call it a date."

"Now that's what I'm talking about." He reached out his hand, palm up, silently asking her for hers. She slid her much smaller hand into his. With their fingers interlaced, his fingertips almost reached the onset of her wrist.

Behind his adorable grin and solid chest, Raddix revealed a loving man whom she didn't want to hurt. The vulnerability in his voice last night, asking her not to break his heart, was something she'd never seen in a man, and it was Raddix's most attractive quality. That, and the way he interacted with Emmanuel. One day, Raddix would be a great dad.

Lily hadn't mentally prepared for the sheriff's questioning. She hated that he was asking her to relive the horror show called her life since getting the first stalker note.

She explained everything to him just as she had Raddix. He held her hand the entire time, drawing soft circles on the back of her hand and wrist. It helped calm her nerves about her situation but ignited every cell in her body, making him more desirable.

"A dead rose? That's what he left with the notes?" The sheriff looked at Raddix and then back at Lily. They were keeping something from her, she could feel it.

"Tell me what you're thinking," Lily ordered, pulling her hand from Raddix.

The men shared another look, harboring very close to Lily losing her patience and telling them both a thing or two.

Sheriff McDugal lifted his hat and placed it back on his head. With dark eyes, he let out a huff. Tired of waiting for the man to speak, Raddix spat out the words, "We found a rose outside the barn the night we were in there, and the attackers struck."

Lily gasped.

"It's okay," Raddix rushed to answer. "He's not convinced they are related, but don't say anything to anyone. That evidence will hopefully be what helps us catch him."

Lily nodded, unable to make her voice work.

"Tell me about your ex-boyfriends," the sheriff continued, apologizing when Raddix let out a low, throaty growl.

She laced their fingers together again, giving Raddix her best you-have-nothing-to-worry-about look. "There isn't much to tell. I had a few typical boyfriends in high school and college who've since married. I've gone on dates, the most recent being a man named River, but nothing serious, and none of them have a stalker vibe."

"River does," Raddix interjected.

"Does River have a last name?"

Lily shrugged. "I'm sure he does, but I never asked. He's the brother of one of my friend's friends. We were introduced long before I ever agreed to go on a date with him."

"Okay. Tell me about your family."

Lily froze. She'd only then realized she hadn't shared all her past information with Raddix. More accurately, she hadn't shared the truth. Fear trickled through her body, wondering if he would be upset.

"What is it, Lily?" Raddix's concerned tone made her feel even more guilty. *It's now or nothing.*

"My name isn't Lily Peters." That he knew. "And my parents and little brother still live in California. They're the ones who convinced me to leave. They didn't want any trouble brought to them."

Raddix's jaw dropped as he withdrew his hand from her.

"Great. She finally found the man she wanted to be with, and she'd blown it by not telling him the truth about her family.

Chapter 31

"Where's Lily?" Emmanuel joined Raddix and Damon at the horse corral.

Raddix hadn't told anyone except Damon that Lily Peters was really Shannon Peters at one time, and that her jerk family sent her away with someone wanting to kill her. He'd been upset at first that she hadn't divulged that information before now, but then anger toward her parents rose in him. He wanted to find her father and punch him in the face a few times to find out how he could send his daughter off like that.

He'd forgotten that Lily wasn't her birth name. But she'd changed her name legally, so she'd always be Lily to him. Damon had talked sense into him, reminding him that he wasn't a girl with someone threatening to kill him, so he had no right to judge even her messed up family.

She'd explained that it slipped her mind to tell him about her family once she told him about the stalker. He made her feel so safe. How could he argue with that?

"She's not feeling well, Buddy, so she's not coming today."

Emmanuel's eyes drooped, and his shoulders sagged. "She broke her promise."

"Did she *promise* you?" People needed a degree to talk with Emmanuel. He remembered every last syllable and held people to what they said or agreed to.

He nodded his head. "I told her that Damon gave me lessons on Tuesdays and Thursdays at ten o'clock. Lily said, "Oh great, I'd love to see you ride Yoshi. Today is Thursday; she should be here."

Raddix could understand the little guy's desire to see Lily. His longing for her ran strong, too. "I hear ya. But based on what you said, it doesn't sound like she *promised*. Besides, sometimes people get sick or must take care of something first."

"That never happens with Amelia. She'd promised to watch me ride one time. She carried the throw-up bucket with her so she could watch me."

"Yeah, well, Amelia had a drive and determination like none other I've seen." Raddix noticed Emmanuel's little nose scrunch up and his lip quiver.

"I want to see my mom," Emmanuel whispered.

Raddix knelt. "Go ahead, Bud, and come back when you're ready."

"Poor guy," Damon shook his head. "I can't imagine anyone being mean to that boy. He's got a heart of gold."

Raddix nodded in agreement. Quinton and Emmanuel had left a ranch in Texas when one of the other kids fiercely bullied Emmanuel.

"Now that Emmanuel isn't hitting on Darlene, all my kids get along great with him," Damon chuckled. "They fight with and love each other like they are biologically related," Damon grunted.

"I can imagine dealing with all that on your own at night must be rough."

Damon lifted his hat and wiped the sweat from his brow. "Some nights are worse than others. I'm grateful we are here. I may not have a wife anymore to help, but I've got all of you who love my kids and want the best for them."

"We love you too, Man," Raddix mocked his buddy, knowing how much he hated touchy-feely conversations. Raddix wasn't big on them either unless he was having them with Lily.

"Thanks," his dry, flat tone made Raddix laugh.

Slapping Raddix with the back of his hand, he said, "Hey, look at that."

Raddix turned just in time to see Alex, Allie, Jeff, Katy, and Quinton exit the butcher shop. The distance kept them from seeing the emotion on their faces, but as their feet dragged away, Raddix knew something was off.

"That's the third time this week I've seen all of them together looking less than happy," Damon said with a conspiratorial tone.

Raddix hadn't noticed since all his attention had been on Lily or getting his chores done so he could see Lily.

"I hope everything is all right," Raddix nodded and waved when Jeff initiated the same gestures.

"Maybe Quinton is trying to hire their replacement, and Jeff and Katy just want to spend as much time as possible with him?"

Emmanuel came zooming from the main house. "You ready now, Buddy?" Damon opened the gate, but Emmanuel climbed the metal fencing and climbed over.

The crunching of gravel underneath tires grabbed the trio's attention.

Excitement raced through Raddix's veins as he jogged toward Lily's car.

By the time he arrived, she'd already parked and slowly walked toward him. He pressed a gentle kiss to her cheek. "It's nice to see you up and around, but—"

"—But what?" She jutted her hip, placing her hand on it for more emphasis. "You better not say I look awful, even if that's true." Her smile, bright as always, ignited a fire in him.

"You could never look awful. Are you feeling any better?" He'd say 'no' based on the sloth-paced walk they were currently engaged in.

"Not really, but I told Emmanuel I'd watch him ride. Then I'm heading back home."

Raddix swooped her up, and her soft squeal lit a small fire in him.

"What are you doing?" She asked, wrapping her arms around his shoulders.

"Getting you to the corral before Emmanuel's lesson ends and Christmas is here."

Lily chuckled softly, playfully whacking him on the shoulder.

"See, Uncle Raddix, Lily is good on her promises." Emmanuel blurted, running toward them.

Raddix swallowed a lump the size of Central Montana so he could speak.

"That's not what I said." He defended himself as he placed Lily's feet on the ground.

Damon spoke up in his defense. "You need the full context for this one."

"I see. One lies," Lily pointed at Raddix, "and the other swears to it." She tossed her thumb over her shoulder toward Damon.

Damon held his palms up, "I don't have any skin in the game; I just thought you might want the full picture." He strode away, taking Emmanuel with him.

Lily rested both forearms on the top rung of the metal fence. Her profile was just as heart-stopping as the rest of her. Her flawless skin glowed even brighter, with the sun illuminating her features.

"How are you *really* feeling? Raddix asked, shifting his body toward her, resting his elbow on the fence.

Lily pressed her forehead into her arms. "Like death. I've called my doctor and explained the situation. He wanted to see me, but I told him I was out of town, so he called me in a prescription, but my insurance wouldn't accept the new prescription at this pharmacy without prior authorization. I had to call them and . . ." she let out a frustrated sigh. "It's been such a hassle. The bottom line is my old pharmacist called this morning to let me know that they sent the prescription to this pharmacy, and I could pick it up later today."

"I'm sorry you have to deal with this," Raddix wrapped his arms around her shoulder and loomed closer, kissing the top of her head.

Lord, please let it be your will to heal Lily. Not for my selfish needs but to ease her pain. Give me the pain if you want, but please take it away from her.

As if she'd heard his prayer, Lily lifted her head and pinned her soft blue eyes on him, making him feel like he was the only person in the world in her eyes.

"I appreciate it. This is your last warning. Life with me might be more sickness than health, so you may want to get out while you can."

Her marriage reference surprised him and must have shown on his face.

Lily chuckled, "Settle down, Raddix. I wasn't proposing, just giving you an out before we got too far along with this."

Lily turned her head when Emmanuel called her. She waved with more energy than Raddix thought she had. Lily Peters was something special, and she was his.

Moving behind her, Raddix wrapped his arms around her waist and rested his chin on her shoulder. Whispering into her hair, he cooed, "I don't want an out. I want you. Always and forever."

Chapter 32

After three days of medicine, Lily finally started to feel better physically.

Knowing that a single rose was left by whoever attacked Big L' Ranch made for a string of sleepless nights, that and the fact that Raddix wasn't there to protect her. Something felt off to her. Lily couldn't pinpoint the problem, but she could tell the Holy Spirit was trying to tell her something.

Sighing inwardly, Lily mentally prepared for her day. She only had Evelyn and Selena this morning. Then, she hoped to steal a nap to prepare herself for the evening session with her millionaire. Raddix and Damon were staking out the east side of the ranch this evening, while Damon's kids stayed at the main house.

Before her patient, she promised to help Violet at the flower shop. The blazing sun shone brightly in the blue sky filled with big, white, fluffy clouds. What she'd give to go for a run right now.

The bell above the door jingled as she pushed the metal handle of the glass door, entering swiftly, but coming to an abrupt stop. She could barely move in this place again.

She spotted Sean behind the counter and worked her way through the crowd to greet him. "Hi, Sean. How are you this morning?"

"Surprised. I came on a different day to avoid all this," he swept his hand across the room, gesturing to Violet's packed store.

"She's on the map now. I don't know if she'll ever have downtime again. I'll free up Violet so she can help you with your order." Lily wanted to ask him who he bought flowers for weekly, but they hadn't had any deep conversations, so she'd ask Raddix to ease her curious mind.

Speaking of Raddix, she'd texted him earlier now that he had his new phone, and still hadn't heard back. He didn't always text back immediately, but this was the longest span. Without his dad at the Ranch, Raddix was probably busy; she wouldn't bother him with more text.

"Hey, Violet. I can take over for you if you'd like to help Sean with his weekly order." The woman's face lit up brighter than the tree in Rockefeller Center at Christmas time. Hopefully, her landlady didn't get hurt. She knew Sean didn't date, ever. Maybe there was hope for him like there had been for Raddix.

As Violet let the customer know there'd be a changing of guards, so to say, she saw the creepy man rush past the front window. Violet had said that he hadn't been in since the first day Lily helped her, but he was here again. Interesting.

Lily still couldn't pinpoint where she'd seen him before, but she knew she had, and it was driving her nuts.

She rushed to the window, but he wasn't anywhere in sight. Perhaps he went into the diner or Outfitters. He could have gone in for a haircut, too.

She texted Raddix again, hoping he'd answer soon.

In the middle of cashing out a lady from the next town over, Lily's memory returned. If that man had short hair, he'd look just like one of the pharmacy assistants from back home. *Could he be my stalker?* She'd had her old pharmacy send her medication to this one. It would have been easy to find her.

"Oh no!" Lily gasped.

"Is everything okay, Dear?"

"I'm not sure." Lily finished the sale, leaving the lady with pleasant parting words, and she rushed to Violet and Sean.

'Raddix isn't texting me back—"

"—He and Damon are staking out the ranch tonight. I'm surprised he didn't tell you," Sean said, confused.

"He did. But he hasn't texted me at all today or responded to my text."

Lily had a few options. She could cancel her upcoming sessions and go to the ranch. She could get the sheriff's number and call him directly, or she could tell Sean and Violet the whole story before the store got busy again.

They were her friends. Heck, Sean could be her father-in-law someday. That warmed her heart, but then she thought about the situation. If her stalker had found her, he'd probably seen her with Raddix. She needed to swallow her pride and get over her embarrassment so these people, her new friends, could help keep her and Raddix safe.

Her throat burned as she swallowed as if she'd swallowed the stem of a rose, thorns and all. "You may want to sit down for this one.

Chapter 33

Her first appointment had come and gone. Evelyn was officially her favorite adult client. Her kind heart was evident in her thoughts and actions, so when she got angry and vented her frustration, Lily encouraged her more than one probably should.

Normally, she would have snuck in a nap, but with Sean sitting in his truck downstairs waiting for her and keeping a lookout, she couldn't sleep. They'd tried Raddix, but Sean couldn't get ahold of him either. Lily prayed, hoping nothing terrible had happened to him.

Lily was packed and ready to go. Her laptop case was next to her, ready for her laptop once she finished with her next client. Sean insisted she stay at the ranch. He told Violet she should come too, but she declined. The woman's reddened cheeks revealed to Lily why she didn't want to. Instead, she was going to say with Mrytle.

Taking a deep breath and slowly releasing it, she prepared for her next client. It was T-minus two minutes before she had to deal with Selena. One good thing was that Selena had requested telehealth for this session. Her name splashed across the top of her screen, but Lily wouldn't let her in early.

The poor woman had so many emotional problems, yet whenever Lily tried to help her with them, she tried to pin the way she was off on someone or something else.

Without Selena having to say a word, it was obvious that she was jealous, like the level Cain was of Abel. Her *Abel* was none other than Amelia Lawrence. If it wasn't Amelia's height, it was her strength. If not for her out-of-this-realm kindness and generosity, it was her ability to move past her mother's death. Lily was still trying to fully understand Selena's feelings of envy regarding Quinton.

She was the epitome of a real-life Barbie doll—blonde, thin, and well-endowed. Her biggest problem was her heart. It led her to say and do evil things.

Selena had lost her mother a couple of years back in a car accident, leaving her alone with her dad. They'd never seen eye-to-eye, but they knew they loved each other. Recently, they'd been fighting more than usual. Selena hadn't told her what her dad's illness was, but he was dying, and if Lily had to guess, Selena was afraid of being alone.

"Hi, Selena, how are you?" Lily greeted her with a smile after letting her into the personal meeting room.

"I'm not very good at all," Selena huffed. My dad is getting sicker no matter what he does. I can't run this ranch. I couldn't even tell you where the checkbook is to pay someone to come do it for me."

Lily bit the inside of her cheek to prevent herself from laughing. She truly felt for the girl, and though Selena had never taken her advice before, Lily was obligated to give it to her anyway.

"Selena. Would it be possible for you to work with your dad to figure out some of this stuff before he gets any worse?"

The blonde basketcase chortled. "He told me, 'You had thirty-plus years to figure this out. How do you expect to learn how to run a ranch now?' He wasn't joking."

What a conundrum! Lily wept for the woman. She clearly couldn't take care of herself, and her dad sounded frustrated, unwilling to teach her at this point.

A loud bang jumped Lily out of her seat. She'd heard it downstairs in Violet's shop. When she didn't hear a cry for help or any other noises, she returned to Selena.

"I should have been better to Raddix." Selena let out an obnoxious sob. "He would have been the best husband."

Lily had wondered how long she'd be able to work with this woman, and tonight was clearly going to be the last night. It wouldn't surprise Lily if she got added to Selena's growing list of people she hated.

Plastering on her most professional smile and digging deep within for a kind, professional tone, Lily said her piece. "Selena, I think finding another therapist to work with is best. I've developed a conflict of interest, and it's unfair for you."

"So the rumors are true. You and Raddix are dating? The color in her face drained.

Lily would never admit that to this woman. "The conflict of interest doesn't matter. It's just important to note that there is one," Lily said with as much empathy as possible.

Selena's tears stopped effortlessly, and her soft, almost whiny voice turned dark, bringing the thin hair on Lily's arms to attention. "I understand."

Did she really? Lily seriously doubted it.

"Well, thank you, I guess. I'm sure I'll see you around town." Then, Selena left the meeting.

Feeling slightly relieved yet more dismayed, Lily ended the meeting and reached for her cell phone. Still, she had not heard from Raddix, making her concern all the greater.

She threw on her shoes, placed her laptop in her bag, and threw the strap over her shoulder. Grabbing the handle of her suitcase, she rolled it behind her. She couldn't believe she was running again, but at least this time, she was running to her future and not away from the problem.

If Raddix hadn't been in charge of the surveillance for the east side of the ranch, she probably wouldn't worry too much that she hadn't heard from him at all today. Who was she trying to kid, of course she would be. What if he and Damon were in trouble?

Sean jumped out of his car, took her bags, and loaded them into her car. "I'll follow you," Sean stated, point blank. Lily locked her car doors, brought the engine to life, and headed toward Big L' Ranch.

Driving underneath the massive Big L' Ranch welcome sign, Lily pulled into a spot on two wheels, figuratively speaking. Her brakes screeched under the force. Hopping out, she whipped her door shut and raced into the main house, Sean quickly on her heels.

"Calm down before you go in there. You don't want to alarm the kids."

Lily nodded, thankful Sean was thinking straight because she hadn't been. During the ride to the ranch, Lily created a whole scene in which she saw Raddix and Damon being held hostage.

The lively dinner conversation was muted when Lily and Sean entered. Everyone stared at her for what seemed like minutes, but it was probably only half a second.

Amelia and Katy rushed to Lily, one on each side, while Sean took Amelia's seat, whispering to Quinton and Jeff.

Quinton stood, moving toward Lily in two quick strides. "I brought them dinner. They were good. Neither of them have their cell phones. They only have the radios to alert us when to call the police or if they need backup."

Sean joined them. "I'm going to drop Lily off at Raddix's. He's not there, and even if he was, my son is a gentleman, so we have nothing to worry about—you know."

He didn't need to tell Lily that Raddix was a perfect gentleman. The night they slept on her couch, he'd been nothing but proper.

"How long are they staying there?"

Quinton spoke up. "All of the attacks happened between eight and midnight, so we decided if nothing happened by one, they would call it a night."

"Are you okay, Lily?"

"I'm okay." She swallowed hard, almost convincing herself that she was. Based on the looks on Amelia and Katy's faces, they weren't convinced.

One thing she knew for sure. Lily would never be okay if anything happened to Raddix.

Chapter 34

"I can't believe you fell that hard." Damon chortled. "Besides me, I thought you'd be the last person to let a woman get to him."

"So you'll never let another woman into your life?" Raddix questioned as he tipped his water bottle back.

"Never really thought about it," Damon admitted. "I mean, I feel bad for my kids, but like I said before, Amelia, Katy, Carolyn, and Renee are amazing mother figures for my children."

"True, but what about you," Raddix continued to grill him.

Damon scoffed, "I'm never trusting another woman ever again with my heart or my kid's hearts."

"Never say never, Man," Raddix snorted. "I said that, and God showed me that He doesn't like that word."

Raddix's initial attraction to Lily had blossomed. Pulling her toward him as if she were the center of Earth and him the unstoppable magnet destined to be in her aura. They'd been interrupted when he tried to converse with her, but her initial reaction scared him.

His mom's death and his dad's neglect had done a job on him, and he knew it. He'd never admit to it out loud, but he was scared they'd leave him if he got too close to someone.

It was only by the grace of God that he turned out the way he did because everyone he was close to as a child had died. Even his dad had neglected him after his mom died.

"Remind me never to get my haircut at this salon again," Damon interrupted Raddix's thoughts.

"What? Why?"

"Willow is on the hunt for a husband. She is looking for an older cowboy from what the Troublesome Trio is spreading." Damon shook his head.

"If my kids ever—"

Raddix busted out laughing, interrupting his friend's words. "I feel bad for your daughters. They are going to lose so many boyfriends."

The thought of losing Lily made him want to hurl. They'd come so far. Lily was finally opening up to him and enjoying time with his family. He knew the "L" word might not be something she could handle at the moment, so he'd keep it to himself, but his feelings were alive and well. He couldn't wait to talk with her tomorrow. He needed to make sure she really wanted to stay in Haven Ridge.

"There won't be any boyfriends for a long time," Damon declared, interrupting Raddix's thoughts. "I'll have to move Darlene far away before she hunts down some older cowboy."

Raddix couldn't imagine himself in California. This had always been his home. In fact, Quinton had already helped him gut the inside of the house Mr. Banks left Amelia, who in turn had gifted it to Raddix. He intended to have Lily help decorate it. In his mind, it would only be a matter of time before he asked her to marry him. She should have a say in the house she'd live in one day, right?

She was seven years younger than him, and maybe she wasn't ready to settle down yet. He couldn't wait until they caught the culprits so he could find Lily and hash these things out.

At one o'clock, Raddix and Damon called it a night and headed back to their cabins.

When Raddix opened his front door, he froze, staring in disbelief as a wide-eyed Lily stared back at him from his couch.

He crossed the threshold and shut the door. "What are you doing here, Lily?" Raddix was by her side in an instant. "Are you okay?"

"I saw the man again, and I think he's from my pharmacy back home, which means when I ordered my meds, he could have followed me here."

Lily moved from one story to the next, telling him about Selena.

Raddix wasn't surprised by Selena's behavior. He called her the she-devil for a reason. The more he thought about the connection between the man and her pharmacy, the more questions he had. She got frustrated the last time he questioned her, but details meant everything.

"Didn't you see that man in the flower shop before you had your prescription sent here?" He treaded lightly, hoping she wouldn't be upset.

Lily leaned against Raddix's chest. "That's not entirely correct. Before I left California, I had to have my regular prescription transferred here, so it's possible he could have been here before me."

"What else don't I know about?" Raddix didn't mean to sound so gruff. "I'm sorry. Lily, I want to know everything about you, especially now, so I can protect you."

"It's okay. Thank you for caring." Lily grabbed his hand, and he let her pull him to his feet. "You should get some sleep."

"No more interruptions, Lily. Tonight, you tell all."

Raddix took a quick shower and brushed his teeth. He couldn't believe Lily was there. He'd surely thank his dad for watching out for her.

When he entered his room, Lily sat on top of the covers in the cutest pink pajama shorts with red hearts scattered all over them. The pink tank top had one big red heart in the center of her chest. *Clothes manufacturers place things in just the right spots to get us men in trouble.*

"You could have covered up," he said, pulling them down for her. "That was sweet of you to make sure you didn't take my side of the bed." He kissed her forehead and then pulled the covers to her chin.

Raddix reached over Lily, and grabbed his pillow.

"Where are you going?

"I'll get a blanket and sleep right down here," Raddix said, pointing to the floor.

Lily bolted upright. "You're not doing that. What's the big deal? We already slept together. . . well, you know what I mean. We slept on the couch together. This bed has more room than the couch."

"Yes, but this is a bed," Raddix stated, figuring Lily would understand his implication.

Lily crossed her arms over her chest. "I get it; the Cowboy is chicken."

"Chicken? What am I afraid of?"

"Beats me. You make almost three of me, so I can't imagine how I'd scare you."

"You may be petite, but you are the scariest thing I've ever faced."

"Are you serious?" Lily's tone told him that she didn't believe she was.

Raddix swallowed hard. "Yes." As soon as he said it, he knew he shouldn't have. She had all the power now, and the smile on her face told him that she knew it, too.

"Well, if you don't sleep on the other side of this bed, there won't be any talking tonight."

"That's blackmail," Raddix argued.

"Take it or leave it," Lily said casually.

She was irresistible. Raddix didn't need the temptation of sleeping beside her to feel that way. It would be blissful torture to be that close to her this evening. Could he tell her that he loved her like this? No, he shouldn't.

"Fine, but I'm sleeping on top of the covers," Raddix announced as he walked around to his side of the bed.

"Well, yeah. You didn't think I'd have it any other way, did you?" Lily laid down on her side, facing Raddix's side of the bed, as he got himself situated.

"So what do you want to know? "Lily asked.

"Anything you want to tell me." Raddix meant that. He wanted to know everything about this woman.

Lily smiled. "My favorite superhero is Iron Man."

"Whoa!" Raddix popped up on his elbow. You aren't going to talk to me like you would Emmanuel, are you?"

"You said *anything.*"

"You're right," Raddix said. "Continue. I'll try not to interrupt."

"I've dreamt of my wedding since I was three. I played basketball for just as long. I was the center for my basketball team in elementary school. By middle school, everyone was taller than me, so I had to change to shooting guard."

Raddix couldn't believe she was opening up to him. He ran his fingers along her bare arm. Should he dare ask about her family? When she continued sharing, he decided it was best to stay quiet.

"My favorite flowers are lilacs. I can't think of anything else. You'll have to ask me questions now."

"Alright."

"Just remember, I get to ask you questions after."

Raddix had his chance. "Tell me about your family."

"There isn't much to tell." Lily sighed. "My younger brother has Cerebral Palsy, so once he was born, I went to the back burner. He had more needs than me, and my parents expected me to help them care for Brandon instead of them taking care of me. When the stalker stuff came about, they told me I should move away. Since Brandon couldn't take care of himself, it wasn't fair to put him in danger."

"That's awful. I'm so sorry." Lily just shrugged at his sentiment.

"Have you ever been in love?' Raddix held his breath, waiting for her answer.

Lily placed her palm below his jaw, warming the skin beneath her fingers. "I've only been serious about one man."

"Lucky guy," Raddix murmured. Feeling confident, Raddix reached for her, resting his hand on her hip.

His mind raced, hoping he didn't regret telling her this and that she returned his feelings.

He slid closer. "Lily?" He shot up in bed. "I need to tell you something, but I need you to promise that you won't run away from me if you're not ready to hear it. I am a patient man."

"This sounds ominous." Lily sat up, too. She set her hands on his shoulders. Rubbing them across his upper back and down his arm. Her hand froze over his bicep.

Tilting his head, he watched her fingers gently caressing his muscles again. The intense look on her face matched the one in his heart.

"If you wanted to feel me up, you could have just asked."

She met his eyes, but didn't stop her movement. "It's not like that. I was just thinking about how you got those muscles."

Lily fixed her gaze on his arm. *Was she pulling away again?* Raddix opened his mouth to say his piece before losing the nerve, but Lily spoke simultaneously.

"Ladies first," he said, barely above a whisper.

"Things have changed for me," Lily paused her words and her hands. "You are clearly a hardworking man," she continued to massage his shoulder and arm.

Raddix wasn't willing to lose her, so he blurted out the only thing he hoped would make the difference.

"I am heart-stopping, death-defying, absolutely in love with you!" He let out a huff a breathe just as he met her eyes that had pools of tears to the brim threatening to flow over.

Chapter 35

"Did you just say that so you didn't have to answer my question?"

"Not at all," Raddix's husky voice did all kinds of things to her insides.

Raddix still hadn't broken his gaze, hypnotizing Lily. Could she take the risk with her stalker so close? No one had confirmed that, but she felt it.

Being around Raddix had given her a new slogan for life: Kiss today, worry tomorrow.

Before she could talk herself out of it, she threw the covers off and jumped onto her knees. Sandwiching one of his legs between hers, she scooted even closer. Placing her hands on either side of his neck, her thumb grazed his ears. "Raddix Lawrence, I am so sorry for putting a target on your back.

It wasn't my intent. But it's only fair I tell you that I am crazy about you, too."

The moment she reached Raddix's firm and attentive lips, he'd already taken control, freeing her from the fear of captivity she'd allowed herself to reside in for so long.

Raddix fell back, bringing Lily down with him. They matched kiss for kiss, forgetting their uneasiness about being beside each other in his bed.

If Raddix hadn't told her he loved her, she would have known it with this kiss. She could feel it in his strong, calloused hands running down her back, gripping her hips. His warm, soft lips slowed, allowing them to catch their breath. His tongue peeked through her parted lips, unleashing a thunderous explosion of emotion within her. She hungered for this—a man who loved her, not one who was obsessed with her and creeped her out.

Lily pulled back. "We need to stop." She rolled back onto her side. She'd kept her virtue for almost thirty years. She wasn't about to disappoint God now.

Staring at his chest, not able to reach his eyes, Lily whispered, "I've never . . . I'm waiting for marriage if that ever happens."

Raddix lifted her chin. "Marriage will happen if I have anything to say about it." She giggled. "As far as the rest, we'll figure it out together."

Excitement bloomed in her chest. "You mean you haven't—"

"—Nope."

"Alright. Let's move away from that subject because you are too tempting."

"Hello, pot, meet kettle," Raddix crooned.

She softly swatted him in the arm. He quickly grabbed her wrist, pulling it to his lips, kissing her palm. "Be careful. Touching my arm is what started everything before."

"True."She pulled her arm back. "Okay, question time."

Lily propped herself on her elbow. This first question is a yes or no one, and the rule is you can't say no."

"That sounds dangerous."

She shook her head. "An amazing cowboy like yourself," she brushed her kiss against his, "You'll be fine."

"You're laying it on pretty thick, so it must be big."

"I'm not sure. But I signed up to help for the festival, and it's my job to get people in the dunk tank."

"Absolutely not."

Surprised, Lily shot up. Staring down at his easygoing expression. She couldn't tell if he was teasing or just adamant he wouldn't do it, so he didn't bother getting excited.

"Come on. You're the first person I've asked. You can't say no."

Raddix smirked. "Well, I might be apt to say yes, if . . ."

"If what?"

Raddix pushed himself up onto one hand. "If I could get one little, itty, bitty kiss."

"Just one?" Lily questioned, leaning closer.

"Yup."

Playing along, Lily brushed his lips with a tender kiss. As she tried to pull back, Raddix captured the back of her head, keeping her lips linked with his.

Lily loved this man. He was playful, tender, and alluring. He was her kryptonite.

When he released her, he declared, "That's definitely worth a dunk in the tank, but only if you can't find enough people."

"Thank you." She skimmed her hand along his jawline; his light stubble felt smooth against her palm. "How is your hair so soft?"

"Coconut oil."

She brought her nose to his jaw and sniffed. "I can't smell coconut."

His boisterous laugh filled her with joy. "I can imagine not. I haven't put any on since yesterday, but it works well."

"Alright, next question. Amelia said she gave you Mr. Banks house and lot. How come you didn't tell me?"

Raddix pressed his back up against the headboard and pulled Lily toward him. Her back pressed against his chest, and Raddix wrapped one arm around her shoulder, resting it on her forearm. They laced their fingers on the other side.

"Quinton has been helping me clean out the man's things. We haven't seen his kids since the funeral and the reading of the will. Amelia said the daughter was so mad that her dad had left the house to Amelia that she didn't even finish listening to the reading of the will. She told Amelia to take care of her dad's things alone."

"I can understand the daughter's feelings, but taking it out on Amelia wasn't fair. How did the son act?"

"Amelia said he was indifferent. He'd stayed to hear that their dad left him the money he had on hand and in his bank. Albeit, it wasn't as much as what the property and house would have sold for."

"Anyway, Quinton and I got everything gutted, and I was waiting to see how you reacted to us before I moved forward with the house."

She stiffened slightly, processing what Raddix was and wasn't saying. "Did I pass the test?"

"For now."

"She whipped her head toward him. What do you mean?"

Raddix brought their laced fingers to his lips and kissed her knuckles. "You said you were crazy about me, which is amazing, but the woman I ask to marry me has to be profusely in love with me."

He had noticed her use of words. She wasn't intentionally not telling him she loved him. Her emotions ebbed and flowed like a rapid white water ride, hence her word usage. *Did he say marry?*

"Marry?"

"Don't sound so surprised, Darlin'. You had to see this conversation coming at some point. Unless I'm way out of sync, I feel like I'm clearly emitting my feelings." He grazed her forearm with his fingers. "You're the only woman I've considered letting in forever. I've never told anyone about my mom's death or my dad's scars. If I'm being honest, I've been terrified that your situation would resolve and you'd head back to California, leaving me behind."

"Not going to happen."

Raddix kissed the top of her head. "I can tell by how you look at me and touch me that you love me, but I need to hear it from you when you're ready."

"Let's make no mistake about this. I am so in love with you; there's no turning back. That's why I keep pushing you away."

"That makes perfect sense," His words dripped with sarcasm. "I'll never understand the woman's mind."

"The creep said he'd kill any man he saw me with and make me watch. I'd rather live without you than watch you. . ." Lily couldn't bring herself to say the words.

"Don't worry about me. I will protect you; this nightmare will be a distant memory."

"Thank you, Raddix. We should get some sleep. I haven't had a complete night's sleep since you stayed at my apartment. I'm hoping to repeat that now."

"You're wish is my command, Darlin'." Raddix shimmied their bodies down to the pillows.

Having his strong arms engulfing her told her what her heart already knew. Raddix was her friend, eye candy, and protector. If they could get past this stalker business, he could even be her husband. Those were the best words Lily had ever heard.

Chapter 36

"Raddix, this is the sweetest thing I've ever seen." Lily breathed.

He hadn't been to his mother's gravesite since her funeral. Looking at her stone did nothing for him. He wanted her live in person to talk to and get the motherly hugs that the women on the ranch tried to replicate for him.

"Who put flowers there?" Raddix wondered aloud.

Lily smiled. "I know, but I don't think it's my place to say."

"Who?" Raddix pushed. "How do you know?"

"I may or may not have witnessed the making of this bouquet." She wrapped her arm around Raddix's waist when he rested his across her shoulders.

Of course. That made sense since Lily helped Violet out as much as she did.

Lily had melted in his arms last night, just like now. He couldn't wait for this mess with her stalker and the property destruction on the ranch to be done. Tonight, he and Damon were going on another stakeout, hoping to catch the culprits this time.

"You don't have to tell me, it's okay. But can you at least answer my questions?" She nodded.

"Is it Amelia?"

"No."

"Katy?"

"Wrong gender."

"It can't be my dad. He won't even talk about her."

Lily silently shrugged her shoulders.

"Seriously?"

She nodded. "He gets new ones every week."

With that information, Raddix stared at flowers. His mouth formed an O, and his eyebrows curved, raising slightly. His dad was the last person he would have expected, but it made perfect sense.

Being here with Lily made it easier for him. Thankfully, Amelia had hired two more ranchhands to help with the horses since Damon knew the most about the orchard and growing products, in case she couldn't find anyone with enough knowledge to replace Alex and Allie.

Today, those new guys worked with Quinton while Damon rested until his afternoon sessions. This Hippotherapy group consisted of five kids with occupational or speech needs. He was great with them, using the horse's movements to improve the kids' neurological functions and sensory disorders. Right afterward, his group consisted of three autistic kids. Emmanuel joined this group when he first came to the ranch. Damon focused on teaching those kids balance, coordination, and core strength.

Emmanuel's coordination and balance improved once he started working with Damon, which made Raddix appreciate his friend and colleague even more.

"Do you want kids?" He asked out of the blue.

"Yeah, but my clock is ticking. I'll be thirty in May." Lily looked up at him. "How about you?"

"Definitely, but like you said, time's ticking."

"Will you take me to see your house?"

"Hop in. Let's go," Excitement burst in Raddix's chest as they drove along the new path they'd formed between the two properties.

Raddix parked in the curved part of the horseshoe driveway. "Wait right there."

He rushed around the front of the truck, opened her door, and held his hand out like Prince Charming. She didn't have a ball gown or glass slippers, but the way his eyes regarded her, she felt like his princess. Her stomach dipped, and her heart thumped against her ribs. Once they reached the top of the stairs, Raddix twisted the knob enough to release the connection and pressed the door open with his foot.

Lily strengthened her grip around his neck, making him all warm inside. That feeling dissipated quickly when the door fully extended. His hand under Lily's legs dropped, careening her feet to the floor with a thump.

"Oh, Raddix. We're never going to get past this."

His statued form couldn't believe the red painted note on his wall.

YOU'LL NEVER ESCAPE ME!

Raddix had taken a shaken Lily back to the main house. They'd called Sheriff McDugal, who rushed over.

"When was the last time you were in the house?" the sheriff asked Raddix.

"Quinton and I went over after dinner last night to see if he'd left his phone there. Nothing was out of place," Amelia spoke up.

"You and Damon will be on the east side tonight, right?" Raddix nodded. "I'm setting Deputy Williams inside the house tonight. This has gone on long enough."

"Thank you," Raddix, Amelia, and Lily replied at the same time.

The sheriff turned to leave.

"Sheriff McDugal," Lily grabbed his attention. "Before you leave, may I ask you something?"

"Sure."

"I'm in charge of getting participants for the dunk tank." His neutral expression turned to a frown quickly. "Would you please go in the tank?"

Raddix loudly whispered near Lily's ear, "You need to stop leading with that line. Just ask quick, so they don't have time to think or react."

"She roped you into it already."

"Of course." *Sort of, but he didn't need to know the specifics.*

"From what I heard, you backed out of the bachelor auction in July, so you really owe it to your community, and I mean, who doesn't want to dunk the sheriff? I bet you'll bring in a lot of money."

"As long as I can go first, just in case I get a call."

"Sure." He knew Lily didn't believe him. "You just don't want to be after the sweaty cowboys."

"Good point. I have to go second then if I'm needed," Raddix stipulated.

Lily agreed, letting the sheriff finally leave.

Right after dinner, Raddix took Lily back to his cabin. I know you won't get any sleep until I get back, but try to rest and don't open the door for anyone. I have my key."

"I love you." Raddix squeezed her tight. Now that he'd told her, he wouldn't stop."

Lily leaned back, and he fell under her spell when her eyes spoke before her mouth. "Raddix, I love you." She pushed up on her toes and captured his lips.

"Pulling back, giving her one last lingering kiss, he said, "I have to go before I don't."

This was ending one way or another tonight.

Raddix set his chair next to Damon. The moon shone brightly tonight, which Raddix had decided would help him see wildlife and perhaps the offenders before they did too much damage. However, the sheriff told Raddix and Damon to make sure the vandals did some damage before they captured them.

"I told you something was up with Alex and Allie. I know they aren't the most pleasant people, but I can't imagine finding anyone who can replace them," Damon said in a whisper.

"I think she did," Raddix said, keeping his voice low. "When Lily and I were at the main house, I overheard Amelia telling Cash and Carolyn they'd have another mouth to feed again."

"Well, that's good. Hopefully, the person has enough knowledge that it doesn't take me away from my horses too much."

"You wouldn't say that if she turns out to be a hot, single blonde." Raddix hadn't known his buddy to date, but his ex was blonde, so he took a guess.

"No, thank you."

There was more silence than talking as the clock hands ticked by.

Just after midnight, Raddix's heavy eyelids bobbed in rapid succession. Suddenly, a noise pulled his attention away, and his stomach lurched. He shook Damon's arm, jolting him awake. Both men armed themselves, Raddix with his Glock 19 and Damon with his shotgun.

The noise drew Raddix's attention to the same post he'd repeatedly fixed the last couple of months. The culprit was trying to kick it like he'd done in the past, but each grunt and kick revealed that the new materials were stronger than the previous.

Damon held the talk button for three seconds and released it. He repeated that two more times. That was their code for Quinton to call Sheriff McDugal. He wouldn't signal back, potentially alerting the criminals of Damon and Raddix's whereabouts. Instead, they had to trust in God that he'd woken Quinton to complete his part of the plan.

Finally, he could get back to Lily and check on her.

They inched closer, Damon on the right of the post and Raddix to the left. About an hour ago, the dark clouds had rolled in, blanketing the night sky. Without the moon's light, they had to rely on their hearing and hope the offender was too distracted to notice them.

"Hey, come help me." the crook kicking at the post holler whispered, stopping Raddix and Damon in their tracks. It was definitely a man's voice—one he'd never heard before.

"What is the problem?"

"They've upgraded their materials."

"Just use the wire cutters if you're too weak to get that done."

She sounds pleasant, Raddix thought.

His thundering heart echoed in his ears. He couldn't wait to capture these two vandalizers. *Wait! What if there are more?*

Raddix hadn't been concerned about their well-being until that moment. There was a little scuffle near the post. Were they fighting with each other? This had to be a married couple.

Raddix groaned inward, wondering when they would hear the police siren—their signal to reveal themselves.

The eerie dark silence of the last minute or two sent Raddix's heart into a full-on tumble. His eyes scanned the black night in the direction where he knew Damon should be. He couldn't even make out a silhouette.

The swift punch and leg sweep came out of nowhere. Suddenly, he was on the ground with a nasty woman trying to claw his eyes out. He covered his face with his forearms like a boxer. *Who was this woman, and where was Damon?*

When there was a break in her slaps and punches, Raddix grabbed the woman's arms and ripped her off him, pinning her to the ground while she filled the night air with a vicious, evil scream.

"You're a thief!" the woman repeated more than Raddix could count.

"Who are you?" Why are you on our property? Well, I know you're destroying it. What I don't know is why."

Finally, he heard the faint police siren. "Damon, where are you?" He wrapped the woman's hand behind her back, securing her hands with a piece of rope he'd prepared in his pocket, and pulled her to her feet.

"Where's your partner? Raddix barked.

She continued to ignore his questions, infuriating him even more.

That, and not knowing if Damon was okay, grated on his nerves.

Just then, he heard the intermittent pulling of something heavy and stopping, releasing a heaving breath and a grunt.

"Damon, is that you?"

"Yeah. This one's not talking," Damon grumbled.

"That's okay. The sheriff has a way of making people talk.

Chapter 37

"Let go of me! You have nothing on us." The woman, whom Raddix referred to as Beast in his head, shrieked, trying to get out of Raddix's grip.

Raddix chuckled. "We caught you destroying our property; you tried to run Lily over and scare her by leaving the rose by our barn."

"You've lost it, Man," The guy Raddix assumed was the beast's husband spoke. "We don't know a Lily—"

"—Stop talking!" Beast's voice, gruff, pushing the man to comply.

Amelia, Quinton, and Deputy Williams met them outside the main house.

"Shirley, Bob?" Amelia questioned. "You've been destroying our property?"

Shirley? Raddix cringed. Her name did not match her personality.

He instantly thought of Lily. Her sweet kindness was a beautiful match for her.

"You know these people, Amelia?" The sheriff asked, surprised.

"They are Mr. Banks's children."

"You stole my father's land and house," Shirley bleated in Raddix's ear.

Fortunately, Amelia and Quinton had told Sheriff McDugal about the will reading and their behavior just in case anything came of it, so he didn't waste any time getting those two in the back of the deputy's car.

Raddix, the sheriff, Amelia, and Quinton watched the deputy drive off. "If they didn't have anything to do with the rose or running Lily off the road, that means—"

"—Let's go." The men hopped in the sheriff's cruiser and raced to the cabin, leaving Amelia behind.

As they approached the door, they saw the still-wet paint sign with streaks running down the door:

SHE'S MINE!

Chapter 38

Lily spied the clock on Raddix's wall—half past one. Raddix was supposed to quit an hour ago. *Why hadn't he come back?*

Lily's wrists burned underneath the nylon rope and zip tie that this monster had attached to her an hour ago. So much for not letting anyone in the cabin. This creep didn't need any help busting the lock on the door, ripping Lily from her thoughts of another restful night with Raddix.

She felt a liquid trickle down her palm. *Must be blood.* If she pulled and tugged to free herself anymore, she might as well rip her wrists completely off. She peeked at her ankles. Those were raw and red, too.

Her mind raced, worrying about whether this creep had already gotten to Raddix as he said he had. If so, did that mean he harmed Damon, too? Lily couldn't imagine more people being hurt because of her.

"What did you do?" Lily's voice boomed with disgust.

The creepo, who had tracked her down from her old pharmacy, pushed his forehead into hers. The mixed smells of coffee and smoke made her want to hurl. Would he hurt her worse if she threw up on him? Probably.

"I saved you from a heartache. That cowboy could never protect you like I can." Lily suppressed a laugh. This lanky creep couldn't save a kitten.

Lily hadn't watched any movies in months, but prior to that, she was an action movie girl. Give her some Jason Statham any time. She imagined herself headbutting this guy and stomping on his instep. The headbutt would probably just irritate this lowlife even more.

She was delusional if she thought she could get out of these ropes and ties like Statham had. She didn't have a grinding saw to cut them off easily, nor did she have a warehouse full of props to throw at her offender. She wouldn't be putting a screwdriver through this guy's hand or kicking him in the face since she didn't have any tools and her feet were tied to this stupid chair.

"I also saved you from having to watch me torture your cowboy." The slow, sinister smile that crept across his face snapped a switch in her brain. She headbutted and spat on him.

As she expected, she was a sitting target since she wasn't Jason Statham, but an inch of pride rose in her chest, watching her captor groan in pain, clutching his forehead.

"If you wanted me to have your spit, you should have said something. I can think of a better way to get it."

The revolting hostage taker pounded his lips to her while she shook her head violently to break free. He clutched her shoulders to keep her still. Lily did the first thing that came to her mind.

With no break in sight, Lily bit his lip.

"You are rougher than I thought. I like it." He brought his hand across his body to his ear. Then, with all his force, he backhanded her.

Lily could have stabled herself, but she dropped to the ground, hoping the chair would break and free her, somewhat.

No luck.

Instead, the side of her head bounced off the floor, sending a thunderous pain through her body that stunned her. Floaties clouded her vision briefly.

His pounding footsteps and her throbbing cheek vibrated against her head. Her left cheekbone might be broken. At the very least, it was swelling quickly, making it difficult to see out of that eye. Blurred black boots grew clearer as they approached.

Please don't kick me in the face. Lily pleaded silently.

Please, Lord, if Raddix and Damon have been hurt, please let Quinton find them and get help. I know bad things don't happen to people unless you let them. What are you trying to teach me? Help me learn it before anything worse happens.

The faint sound of a police siren grew louder and louder. Had she hit her head that hard? Was she dreaming, or was help really coming for her? *Thank you, God!*

Her captor yanked her up by the arm and screamed in her face. "Did you call the police?"

Seriously? Was he nuts? She already knew the answer to that rhetorical question.

He may be lanky, but he was stronger than Lily. Despite scratches and the one good punch to the nose she got in before he subdued her, he had her under his control pretty much from the beginning. When would she have called the police?

"They are on to you. When you left a rose by the barn, I had to tell them that was your signature. Then you tried to run me down with a car. Did you really think you could get away with this forever?

Her imprisoner paced. Lily's nervousness grew as he escalated. "I didn't leave a rose near any barn. I haven't been on this property until I followed you and that man here from your apartment."

Sean. Lily hoped this guy didn't hurt Raddix's dad.

Was he telling the truth? If so, then who left the rose?

"He pulled a gun from his waistband and started waving it around like a maniac when he heard a noise outside.

Pulling the curtain back, he groaned. "Your cowboy and the sheriff are outside.

On impulse, Lily smiled. Wrong thing to do.

The deranged man forced the gun into her jaw. "Smile again, and I'll blow your brains out and make him watch. Do you understand?"

Lily shook her head. Her entire body trembled. She'd done well to keep her tears stifled, but she lost the ability, and drops fell from her eyes.

The police department in this town consisted of two men. They were unprepared for this situation, and she brought it to them. Maybe it would be better if he eliminated her, taking away the only trouble this town had ever seen. These good people did not deserve this peril.

"Lily. We are here. You'll be okay." Hearing Raddix's voice, though muffled through the door, had a starburst effect on her heart. "Lily, call out. Let me know you're okay."

With the gun shoved back in her face, Lily stiffened. "Don't you say a word!" Venom dripped from her captor's fangs.

He pressed his back up to the wall right next to the door, the wobbling gun pointed at her. "Don't you talk to my girlfriend. She's mine!"

"You are sadly mistaken, Fella. That beauty, who better not have a scratch on her, is mine," Raddix's words filled Lily with joy. She never thought she'd have a man calling her *his*, but Raddix had proved her wrong.

His voice became clearer and louder. *Was he moving closer? Get back, Raddix.*

Lily instinctively turned to her left when she heard a noise. Someone, presumably Raddix, knocked on the front door at the same time, jumping the gunman yet keeping his attention on the front of the cabin.

"Back up, or you'll be wiping her brains off your wall."

"Drop the gun," the sheriff's voice boomed to Lily's left as the front door fell off its hinges when Raddix kicked it in.

Within seconds, Lily screamed, but Raddix pushed her out of the way. The stalker swung the gun in Raddix's direction. Raddix grabbed the man's wrist and the top of the gun, shoving it downward. He banged the guy's hand off the side table until the gun fell to the ground. Pointing straight at Lily, thankfully it didn't misfire.

Raddix wrestled him to the ground, exchanging punch for punch, all the while the stalker screamed, "I love her! She's mine! Get off me!" Raddix's last punch knocked the man unconscious.

Her real-life Jason Statham, but oh so much better.

Raddix released Lily from her ties and pulled her to his chest. Once she reached his warm embrace, more tears fell. "You saved me," she choked out. Thank you."

Raddix kissed her forehead. "You didn't think I would let him take you, did you?

"No, but he said he didn't leave the rose, so that means there's still danger."

He stroked her hair. "Don't worry, Darlin', we've got some answers on that front too."

"Only some?" Lily sighed, letting her head flop onto his chest in defeat.

Chapter 39

Two days hadn't been enough time for Lily to deal with what had happened. Raddix realized that psychologists get their own therapists to talk with. He was happy that Lily wasn't one of those stubborn people who said they could handle things on their own.

He hadn't gotten Lily to step back into his cabin, so he needed to fix up the house even faster. They'd gone to Outfitters and gathered materials early so they could have the majority of the day to get the house where they wanted it.

"Where'd the painted message go?"

"Quinton painted over it for us, so you didn't have to see it again," Raddix explained.

"I'll be sure to thank him." Lily's frown worried Raddix.

"What's wrong?" He took hold of her hands.

Tears welled in her eyes, causing Raddix to wince. He hated seeing her cry. Maybe he shouldn't have said anything.

"I've never known what it was like to have people-err family care about me. I mean, Quinton barely knows me, and he took the time to make life easier for me when I'm sure he has plenty he can do with Emmanuel and Amelia."

"True, but everyone takes care of everyone here. If I were you, I'd be careful. You may have some people looking for free advice."

Lily waved her hand dismissively. "I'd help anyone out on this ranch. Anyone in this town, probably."

"I heard through the grapevine that you dismissed Selena from your case-load," Raddix said without judgment.

She groaned and covered her face with her hands. "I can't reveal anything, but I don't want you anywhere near that woman."

Raddix liked her protectiveness over him. "I wouldn't wish Selena on my worst enemy, so trust me when I say I do everything I can to stay clear of her."

He walked Lily backward until she bumped up against the wall. "Your jealousy is kinda sexy."

"I'm not jealous," she proclaimed. "I just know she means to cause trouble, and we've had enough.

We've?

This was the first time Lily had referred to them as a couple. At least it was the first time Raddix's brain registered the comment, and he liked it.

Placing one hand on the wall next to her head and the other firmly on her hip, he boxed her in, pinning her warm eyes with his. Her long, blonde hair was pulled back in an elastic, exposing her jawline and neck, pleading for him to warm her with his kisses.

"I can't hear your words, but everything else is asking me to kiss you. If I'm reading you wrong, you'll have to stop me."

Raddix closed the gap between them centimeter by centimeter, giving her ample time to object, which he hoped she didn't.

She tugged at the hem of his shirt. Lily held his gaze as her warm hands reached under it, leaving a fire trail on his skin. She wrapped her hands around his waist and up his back.

"You can stop asking if this is okay. I want nothing more than to be in your arms for as long as you'll have me."

"How does forever sound?"

"Perfect."

Black filled the night sky before they wrapped up their work.

"We kicked butt today." Raddix high-fived Lily. She wasn't just the woman he loved and would marry. She was his friend. The one with whom he shared his inner thoughts and dreams. He started to see that she felt the same way.

"Once you move your stuff from the cabin to here, it will be official."

"Lily, I don't want to move in here until we move in together."

He couldn't quite read her expression. "Is that a look of panic or happiness?" He asked, hoping for the latter.

"Both," Lily admitted. "Panic because I'm not going to move in with you unless we're married and happy for the same reason, if that makes sense."

He laughed, pulling her into his embrace. "I thought I was the one afraid of commitment?"

"You are," she stated flatly, getting him to laugh. "I'm not afraid of commitment. I'm nervous. What if I'm not a good wife or not what you expected?"

"Impossible." Raddix laughed. "I never thought I'd be the sound of reason in this relationship." He brushed his lips against hers, tasting the strawberries they had for a late snack. "I want you, flaws and all. I'm sure you have some; I just haven't figured them out yet."

She giggled and rolled her eyes. With a mind of their own, his knuckles caressed her cheek. "I've never been a husband, so I'm sure I'll mess up too. But I'd rather mess up with you than be without you."

"Oh, Raddix." Lily pulled him in for a lingering kiss. Her soft, plump lips danced perfectly with his, kindling the fire throughout his body that she'd set earlier. Her lilac scent filled his senses when he breathed her in, eliminating the paint fumes.

She leaned into him more and let out a little moan, driving him impossibly closer to her. An abundance of time passed while he kissed Lily. He may have taken control of this kiss, but she had a meticulous hold on his heart.

Their phones buzzed at the same time, pulling them apart, albeit very slowly.

"We should throw those things in the creek."

Lily just giggled as she turned away from Raddix.

"What's up?" Raddix answered his at the same time. "Okay. We'll leave now."

Raddix waited for Lily to finish her call. The look on her face was one of pure concentration mixed with determination.

"Yeah, do anything that keeps Raddix and me safe. Well, and everyone else at the ranch and in town, too," she added, letting her eyes roam over him. "Yeah, I know, but I'm the lucky one."

Her eyes connected with his, and Raddix knew right then that he needed to speed up his plan.

Chapter 40

Raddix had been acting off the last few days. Unfortunately, Lily hadn't brought it up, thinking it would blow over. Besides, she'd been busy with her client list, which had almost doubled. The people in this town loved to talk.

Once they'd found out her situation, they were right there to support her. Some of the women Lily knew were just helping her grow her business since they shared most of the information they talked to Lily about with the entire town anyway.

"Thank you very much. The firetruck will be along soon to fill it. You'll be back tomorrow to pick up, correct?" Lily confirmed with the men from the church who dropped off the dunk tank.

Everything had been set up yesterday for the End of the Summer Festival, except for the dunk tank. Lily couldn't believe she'd gotten so many people to participate.

Cora also said I should find someone else to fill my role next year since I won't be new in town, and they probably won't be as generous help.

Lily didn't believe that for a second. The people of this town were kind-hearted and generous to everyone.

"T-minus three hours, and the gates will open up. I can't believe Labor Day is Monday. Where did the summer go?" Willow strolled up to Lily.

"I have it under good authority that you are in charge of the dunk tank order. Is that correct?"

"Yes," Lily hesitated.

Willow stuffed her hands in the front of her sweatshirt. "Care to share when the sheriff will be in the tank?"

She shrieked when her new friend began rocking on her heels. "You're interested in the sheriff?"

Her pink cheeks told Lily all she needed to know. "So you're going to dunk him? Aren't the guys supposed to be the ones who do things like that?"

Willow shrugged. "Please don't say anything. I've had a crush on him for years, like when it wouldn't have been appropriate, but now we're adults. My parents are pushing me to date more to find the one." She rolled her eyes at the thought, and Lily laughed.

"Do you think you have a harder time dating because your dad's the pastor?" Lily wondered aloud.

"Probably. Especially when he tells them not to touch me below the neck; only husbands get to touch lower." Her mocking voice had Lily gasping for air.

"Oh my," Lily burst out laughing. "That's not funny. I'm sorry." She composed herself. "I can imagine the word 'husband' scares most men away—"

"—On a first date, yeah!" Willow nodded. I'm glad he watched out for me. Back when he had to give those talks, there were a lot of traveling cowboys, so it was a valid conversation. But Gerard has had my attention for years."

"Gerard is his name?" Lily asked.

Willow smiled. "Please tell me you didn't think his first name was Sheriff."

"Funny. I guess I'd never heard his name and had no reason to ask. But now, all I can think of is Gerard Butler." Lily pondered that for a minute. "I can see the comparison. Strong, saving people, handsome. . . of course not as handsome as Raddix." Lily stated adamantly, causing them to giggle.

"Be here right at nine. I'll try to hold everyone off and let you go first. He promised me thirty minutes before he patrols the grounds."

"Thank you. You're amazing." Willow jogged off, probably to do her hair and perfect her already flawless appearance.

The closer it got to opening the gates to the public, Lily watched with the utmost respect as people set up their booths and brought in their animals.

Raddix and his dad had arrived an hour ago with their cattle and Damon with his horses. She'd never watched Raddix actually work before now. He was impressive. The cattle listened to him, mostly. Every movement he made was intentional. He might have tried to impress Lily with a few more flexes, but she would never complain. Before returning to her work, she gave him a steadfast kiss, promising to return as quickly as she could.

"Save a dance for me," Raddix requested.

Lily's hand slid down his cheek. "I'll save all the dances for you." She winked at him, and he grabbed his chest like he was dying. *Emmanuel was right; he does that often.* But she liked it. She loved everything about him.

When she passed the horses, Lily hollered, "Damon, don't forget you're in the tank at noon." He nodded, acknowledging her reminder. One, she knew he'd rather forget, which made him an even more impressive man for helping out.

Walking back to the dunk tank, she journeyed through the food booths, stopping to talk with Katy and Jeff.

"Hey. How are you guys holding up?" Alex and Allie left two days ago. Katy's previously red-rimmed eyes were more pink today.

Katy smiled. "Getting through."

"I hope he knows what he's doing?" Jeff's gruff voice boomed from behind his wife's head.

"Well, if he doesn't, hopefully, he knows that he can always come back."

"We've told him such, and so did Amelia." Katy set up her cash box in the middle of the table.

"Between you and me, Amelia said she thinks there's a bigger problem, but Axel wouldn't admit anything to either of us." Katy pointed at her chest and threw her thumb over her shoulder, gesturing to her husband.

"Amelia's already filled their position. If she fits in at the ranch, Amelia will never get rid of her, so those two would have to play nice if they returned," Jeff declared as he set up his row of grills.

"Yeah, Harlyn will be here to help me out soon. Hopefully, you get a chance to meet her," Katy declared.

"I don't think we will have any downtime today, but feel free to send her over and introduce herself. I am excited to meet her."

Willow was the first one in line, and she about melted under the last of the warm Montana sun rays when the sheriff took off his shirt and climbed the small ladder to situate himself on the collapsable bench.

"Breathe girl. You won't be able to dunk him if you pass out."

"Come one, come all. Who wants a chance to dunk the sheriff? Remember that pesky speeding ticket he gave you? How about you younger ones? Has he ever kicked you off abandoned property? Here's your chance to feel better about that."

"Hey, the line is long enough. I'm only here for thirty minutes, so you should stop gathering more participants who'll be sad if they don't reach the front of the line.

Willow threw the first ball. She was way off. Lily told her to look at her target, not his bare chest, and she might do better.

"Easier said than done," Willow breathed.

The second ball nicked the target, and the sheriff wobbled. "Not bad. Willow. Maybe you should spend more time honing your throwing skills instead of hiding in your hair salon all day.

"Hiding? Who's hiding? Where can the people of Haven Ridge find you regularly? It certainly isn't patrolling or at the station."

Where had this come from? Lily was utterly confused by their comments. "Are you guys just joking?" She whispered in Willow's ear.

"Nope. I forgot to mention that we don't really get along too well. He's been a jerk for as long as I can remember, and I give it right back."

"Hmm. Interesting," Lily smirked.

"What?"

"Sounds like your feelings might not be one-sided."

"Yeah, right." Willow's words sounded defeated, but her tone and expression were hopeful.

"Tonight, Willow." The sheriff hollered from the tank.

She wound up, and the ball hit its mark. The sheriff went in with a splash. Then she sashayed her way toward the sheriff.

"The next time you think about giving me grief, beware. I have many talents you aren't aware of."

The oohs and ahhs that escaped the next few guests in line were loud and unmistakable.

Lily studied the sheriff for a few moments. His eyes hadn't left Willow. She couldn't tell exactly where his eyes were landing on the woman as she sauntered away, but his cheeks were pink when he realized Lily had caught him. She gave him a knowing smile. He just shook his head and took his position back on the bench. Lily would have to ask Raddix about that combo.

Chapter 41

I t'd been a successful day. Damon got caught up with his horses and couldn't help Lily at his scheduled time, but he sat proudly on the bench, shirtless and probably cold as the sun drifted low behind the trees.

Raddix sat on the boulder protruding from the ground while Lily gave the next participant their softballs, hoping they would dunk Damon.

It was then that he noticed his friend's eyes peak. Raddix turned to see a redhead strolling toward the booth. Damon's eyes never left the woman, who stuck out her hand.

"Hi, I"m Harlyn. Katy told me to introduce myself. You must be Lily."

"I am, and this is Raddix," Lily said, walking back to him and putting her arm around his shoulders.

Lily kept one eye on the kiddo, trying to dunk Damon while continuing her conversation with this new woman. *Impressive.* Raddix could only focus on one thing at a time.

"Hi, guys!" Emmanuel hollered as he approached with Reneé.

When Harlyn turned and smiled at him, Emmanuel stepped right up next to Raddix's shoulder.

"It's nice to have you back. Hopefully, Rocco got a lot of rest. Those newborns are ready for him."

"We did. Thank you."

"Renee, this is Lily, my girlfriend. Lily, Reneé." That was the first and the last time he'd introduce her as such.

They exchanged pleasantries, and then it was Lily's turn.

"Amelia just hired Harlyn to take Axel and Allie's place," Lily explained.

"Nice to meet you," Renee stuck out her hand for Harlyn to shake.

"Likewise."

"Can I dunk my dad?" Dean asked with an ear-to-ear grin, tossing one of the balls in the air.

"Remember who pays your allowance, Son," Damon yelled from his perch.

Raddix leaned over and whispered, "If he cuts you off for knocking him in, I'll make sure you get your allowance."

Raddix handed Lily a fifty for the cash box. "All of you can sink your dad."

"Payback is coming," Damon pointed at Raddix, who laughed at the shirtless man mere moments away from getting dunked by young children.

"Is my dad going in the tank?" Emmanuel asked with the most excitement Raddix had ever seen him have.

"No, I'm sorry, Buddy."

Emmanuel shrugged his shoulders, and they sagged along with this head. "That's okay."

Renee and Lily looked at each other with sad eyes. Emotion pulled at Raddix. He knew Quinton would do anything for his kiddo, but this was the first time Emmanuel had shown any interest.

Dean only had one ball left, and when he saw it wasn't going to hit its mark, the kid bolted to the target and pushed the arm, busting a gut when his dad sank beneath the water.

"My turn!" Dominic jumped up and down.

Dominic and Darlene resorted to their brother's strategy, dunking their dad two more times.

Harlyn had drifted off, talking with Willow at the next booth, who was braiding a girl's hair.

Clearly still hung up on Lily's introduction, she returned to ask, "Amelia hired one person to fill two people's positions? I'm flattered, but like I told her, I haven't used my agriculture degree in almost a year."

"I'm sure if Amelia hired you, she thinks you're capable," Raddix spoke up. "Besides, Damon will be there to help you. He has his degree in agriculture, too."

"Phew. That's a relief. Where can I meet Damon."

Raddix slowly lifted his finger, pointing toward the tank. Damon had emerged from his last dunk. "That's it's my time is up, right, Lily?

"He's Damon?" A few shades of pink rose on Harlyn's cheeks.

Raddix and Lily shared perceptive smiles with Renee, who ushered the kids to the next activity.

"Don't worry, he wears a shirt in the winter. They're pretty cold around here," Raddix joked, earning him a loving swat on his shoulder.

"Stop it, Raddix. Come on," Lily said as she guided the woman toward the tank when the boy threw his last ball at the target.

"Damon, this is Harlyn. Amelia hired her to fill Axel and Allie's position, so you two will work closely together."

Silence.

Lily urged in a loud whisper. "This is where you say, Nice to meet you, Harlyn." Maybe shake her hand, something."

Raddix watched in amazement, or maybe grief. Lily would fit right in with the Troublesome Trio, who were trotting their way.

"Lily." He tilted his head toward the determined ladies.

She chuckled. "You better wipe those looks off both your faces, or those harmless looking grandmas are going to have a field day with you!"

Under the stars, dancing with Lily was where he wanted to spend the rest of his life. The smell of her coconut suntan lotion, of the soft, flowery conditioner, was intoxicating. It gave him peace and calmed his nerves that had spiked the last hour.

"Do you want to take a break?" Lily asked.

"No," Raddix growled.

Lily jerked back.

"I'm sorry. I want you to myself, and the only place that will happen is on the dance floor."

"That's sweet." Lily nuzzled her head back onto his chest, and he breathed a sigh of relief.

Amelia was always in charge of the community dances. He finally locked eyes with her, lifting his eyebrows, questioning when *their* song would play.

He watched her whisper something to the disc jockey and then gave him a thumbs up. *Finally. Alright, now give me the words, please, Lord."*

"Are we done dancing now?" Lily asked when the music stopped.

"Depends."

"Are you okay, Raddix? You're acting weird." Lily studied him. He felt the sweat building underneath his hat. If the music didn't start soon, he might throw up. *Was she ready for this?* He was? If she rejected him . . .

Fortunately, the first few beats pushed through the speakers. "Nope. I love this song."

"This is *Perfect* by Ed Sheeran. You know this song?" Lily questioned.

"You do remember how many women work on the ranch, right?" Her giggle vibrated through his chest.

He held her hand close to his chest, but he captured her eyes and sang the song's first few lines to her when they started.

I found a love, for me.

Darling, just dive right in and follow my lead.

Well, I found a girl, beautiful and sweet,

Oh, I never knew you were the someone waiting for me.

Raddix released her and slowly descended to one knee. Lily's eyes filled with tears, and her hands covered her open mouth.

"Come on, Lil, I haven't even said anything yet." His tone was teasing. At that moment, his heart swelled, knowing how she'd answer.

A tear fell as she shrugged her shoulders.

Emmanuel came running over to hand him the ring box. Typical Emmanuel style: He loudly whispered to Lily, "Please say yes. I'd hate to see him die right here. He told my dad he'd do that if you said no."

Lily let out a laugh mixed with tears, quickly wiping them from her cheeks.

Raddix turned Emmanuel's shoulders in the direction he came. "Thank you, Emmanuel. Now head back to your dad."

The music lowered, and everyone in town gathered. The troublesome Trio had camera flashes going off. Raddix felt like he was on the red carpet, not in Central Montana trying to propose to his girlfriend.

"Lily, you have changed me. I've been waiting my whole life for you and didn't even know it. You're the woman I want to wake up next to every day for the rest of my life. I'll protect you, honor you, and love you. I know what love is because of you. Will you do the honor of marrying me?"

She nodded, and tears flowed down her cheeks like a river escaping a dam.

"I'm going to need a verbal confirmation, Darlin'," Raddix teased.

"Yes," she squeaked, pulling Raddix to his feet and capturing his lips.

"Someone's excited to have her cowboy," he teased her more.

"Shut up and kiss me," Lily ordered playfully.

"With pleasure." He pressed a lingering kiss to hers.

Nothing could upset him right now. They finished dancing to the rest of the song while everyone in town wished them the best.

Then, a throat cleared behind them.

He'd spoken too soon. Selena's presence was a black cloud. "Can I talk to you two, please?"

Selena clasped her hands in front of her. "First off, congratulations are in order. You guys make a great couple."

That was the most forced compliment he'd ever heard, but he didn't care if she was happy with their relationship or not.

"I need to tell you both something that will make you," she pointed to Raddix, "hate me even more, and Lily, you'll probably start hating me once you hear what I have to say."

"Go on." Raddix urged.

"I tried to come between you both. I had someone place a rose outside one of your horse's barns, knowing you'd find it and maybe come running back to me."

Anger began to rise in Raddix's chest. He'd been so sure that Lily's stalker left the rose on his property that he hadn't considered anyone else. Had that made it easier for her stalker to attack? He clenched his free hand into a tight ball.

"When you didn't, I tried to scare Lily away. I never planned on actually hitting her with the car."

"That was you!?" Raddix lunged forward before he could stop himself.

Selena flinched and stepped back. He'd never hurt a woman, but he couldn't deny wanting to at the moment.

"You are sick!" Raddix yelled. Lowering his voice, her ordered, "Stay away from me, and you best stay away from Lily.

"I'm sorry," Selena whimpered.

"I forgive you," Lily said without hesitating.

"What!?" Raddix snapped.

"She almost killed you and tried to tear us apart," Raddix defended his anger.

Lily placed a soft palm on his chest. "But she didn't, and she's owning up to her mistakes now."

Turning to Selena, Lily smiled. "Thank you for being honest. I hope you'll see your worth one day and become a positive member of this community."

"Thank you, Lily," Selena whispered as she walked away, leaving the newly engaged couple to themselves.

"Have I told you what an amazing woman, you are, Lily Peters?"

"Not today, but I'm all ears," she urged, leaning closer.

Raddix brushed his lips against Lily's. "I plan to, every day for the rest of my life."

He took his hat off his head and placed it on hers.

"You are mine, girl." Raddix pulled Lily's hips tight to him. He snuck underneath the hat—*his* hat on her head and seized her lips.

Pulling back a centimeter, Raddix felt her breath mesh with his. "I love you, Lily. Thank you for agreeing to spend your life with me."

Her ardent expression and warm hands lit a fuse in his chest.

"No thanks necessary. You are the love of my life. I can't wait to start my life with you."

"That's great to hear. That means you won't make me wait too long to call you my wife."

"Definitely not."

Their lips crashed together, sealing their love and future with a kiss.

Unedited Chapter from The Perfect Match

Everyone had finally cleaned up the kitchen, and Damon lingered, needing to speak with Amelia and Quinton about a problem on the ranch.

"Dad, do we have to go right to bed?" Darlene asked.

"You can hang out with the other kids while I talk with Amelia and Quinton."

She ran into the living room. Damon smiled when she announced, "Dad said we can play for a while."

Damon loved living and working at Big L' Ranch. His mind flitted between questions and concerns about the newest employee. Typically, he didn't involve himself when it came to his colleagues, but this one was different.

Harlyn Summers was trouble with a capital T. He had reservations about her from the moment he met her. Sitting perched on the bench in the dunk tank a few weeks back, she strolled up, introducing herself to Renee, Raddix, and Lily.

He thought he could work with her, considering she proved well-versed in agriculture. She even turned out to be a reputable photographer who'd already won over the hearts of Darlene, Dominic, and Dean, his three children, who enjoyed their pictures taken.

His reluctance had nothing to do with her work ethic or knowledge of cultivating and growing crops.

Just thinking about her rosy pink cheeks, smooth-looking lips, and curvy hips that were in his hands earlier that day . . . *Focus.* He cleared his throat, hoping no one was paying him any mind.

Working at the ranch had been the best thing that had ever happened to him. His children had other kids to play with, and Renee, the veterinarian's wife, homeschooled all the children. Damon had other adults to interact with, and he worked with horses all day.

Now that Harlyn had invaded his space, things were meek at best. She caused mayhem to run through his head and adrenaline to flow through his veins.

He'd promised himself he wouldn't bring another woman into the kids' lives since their mother, Cheryl, left them all. She blamed Damon, accusing him of choosing his career over her, thus ripping the family apart.

That had been eight years ago. Darlene, his oldest was only two when Cheryl left. Her manipulation didn't fool Damon. She didn't like the country.

After his parents died in a plane crash on their way home from his competitions, she thought Damon would up and leave the sport and the ranch. When he didn't, she got mad and left.

When everyone else left the kitchen, Damon said, "Amelia, Quinton, one of you needs to do something about Harlyn."

"What is the problem?"

She's too sweet and attractive—a major distraction, pushing me to my limits.

"Damon?" Quinton pulled him back into the conversation.

He crossed his arms over his chest. "She's going to finish the tilling and greenhouse work, and then we'll be set until spring. Do you have plans for her throughout the winter?"

No, Damon, she's leaving, and you won't see her until spring. He answered for them. *Great. No, that isn't good. Shut up!* He admonished himself.

"We discussed the schedule she needs to keep for the greenhouse crops, but the rest of the time is hers. She mentioned taking pictures of the Rockies, so I imagine she'll travel around and work on building her portfolio or submit more photos. Did you know she won a Prix Pictet for one of her pieces?"

Damon could tell by the mischievous look on Quinton's face that he'd read Damon's mind. The man knew Damon's problem with Harlyn Summers, the person, not the agricultural specialist or photographer.

This kind-hearted, attractive woman interfered with his ability to focus on his job. The last thing he needed was to get into the corral with a wild stang and get stomped to smithereens because she'd taken up permanent residency in his mind.

Yep, this was his problem, and the smiling fool in front of him wouldn't help. All those times Damon had razzed Quinton about having the hots for Amelia the second she opened the door for his interview were coming back to haunt him.

He sat quietly for a moment, thinking about how much to reveal. He couldn't tell them her sweet, melodious voice punched him in the gut every time she sang a line or chorus of a song; some he knew, and some he didn't, but they all sounded great coming from her.

If she was going to remain on the ranch. *Wait. Where was she living?*

"So she's residing here on the ranch?"

"Yes. She took Raddix's old cabin since he moved into his house."

That's three hundred feet away from his. "Great." Even he could hear the sarcasm dripping from his response.

"Hey, Dad! Dean came barreling into the kitchen. "Harlyn wants to take our pictures on top of our horses tomorrow. Isn't that great?"

Just then, the woman in question turned the corner, and they locked eyes. Her silky red hair rested against the front of her shoulder, and her full, pouty lips called his name.

He stood abruptly, the chair falling behind him. "That's great. It's time to get ready for bed. There's school tomorrow. Let's go."

"Are we done here?" Quinton asked with a grin.

"Yep." Damon was definitely done.

How About a Review?

Your feedback is valuable, so please consider sharing your thoughts. This will help other readers discover this book and my other works.

Thank you from the bottom of my heart for reading and reviewing my book(s).

Amazon

Goodreads

Bookbub

Acknowledgements

"And whatever you do, whether in word or deed, do it all in the name of the Lord Jesus, giving thanks to God the Father through him." ~ Colossians 3:17

This book would not have been possible without The Good Lord's support and encouragement. It may be cliché, but I believe it wholeheartedly!

To my family—thank you for adapting to writing schedules, critique groups, and constantly having a notebook and pen in my hand. I love you guys!

To my IG/Bookstagram friends—you are the best community and I am blessed to be a part of it. Thank you for welcoming me with open arms and being there to support me.

To all beta and arc readers—you are invaluable! THANK YOU for your support. Being an indie author is hard, and your support and encouragement are invaluable.

To all my readers—Saying "Thank you" is just not enough! With all the possibilities you have, you read The Perfect Cowboy. It's an honor that you chose one of my books to read. Without you, I wouldn't be an author. Thank you for bringing me along into your life. Until we meet again...

About the Author

Karen Tucci, a public school teacher by profession, now tutors writing students online and homeschools her two children.

A native of Maine, she has trekked miles of the Pine Tree State and visited countless others. It is through her life experiences that the basis for her romance stories develop. One of her favorite things to say when out adventuring is, "...that is definitely going in my next book!"

Fun fact: Karen had only read and wrote non-fiction growing up. It wasn't until her late twenties that she embraced the joy brought forth by doing both — reading and writing — within the different romance tropes. Now she reads at least fifteen fiction novels a month and writes daily!

Connect with Karen:

Facebook Reader's Group.

To find out about special deals, giveaways, and new releases, join her newsletter:

https://www.trueheartromance.com

Instagram

Goodreads

Bookbub

Amazon

www.ingramcontent.com/pod-product-compliance
Lightning Source LLC
Chambersburg PA
CBHW020143310726
48970CB00006B/1986